EVERY BUSH IS BURNING

EVERY BUSH IS BURNING

BRANDON CLEMENTS

TWISTED BEAM
PRESS

Every Bush Is Burning
Copyright 2011 by Brandon Clements. All rights reserved.
ISBN 978-0-9837850-0-2 (paperback). Also published in hardcover and
eBook formats.
Published by Twisted Beam Press.

Printed in the United States of America.

This is a work of fiction set in Columbia, SC, but there are real places,
musicians, businesses, and organizations mentioned. Any churches described by the main character in a less than positive light are not intended
to reflect actual churches in Columbia. Though the main characters are
entirely fictitious, there are some side characters who are real people and
friends of the author. Their real names have been used with permission.

Though Brandon works as a pastor at Midtown Fellowship, the views
presented in this book are solely his and are not intended to reflect on the
organization of Midtown Fellowship.

Developmental Editing: Andy Meisenheimer (andymeisenheimer.com)
Cover Design: Kent Bateman (kentbateman.com)
Trailer: Dust of the Ground Media (dustground.com)
Website: Stephen Bateman (stephenbateman.com/connect)

For you.

You know who you are.

To the hard of hearing you shout, and for the almost blind you draw large and startling figures.

—Flannery O'Connor, *Mystery and Manners*

1

I must ask you in advance to forgive me, because I imagine this letter will catch you off guard. I'm about to break a social norm or two here. The thing is, I've been sitting here watching you for forty-five minutes. I've sat here and watched you drink your french roast from that orange mug while you nibble on your crumb cake and read your book. I'm thinking about how I've been a regular at this coffee shop for years, and how you've also been a regular as long as I can remember. And I don't think I have ever spoken a word to you. I have no clue what your name is. To be honest, you've always just been another body making the line longer for me, or taking the table I want—the good one right next to the outlet.

Forgive me. I am maddeningly self-centered. But at least I'm starting to realize it. Unfortunately, the main thing I'm consumed with when I'm sitting somewhere like a coffee shop is how I am perceived. Do people think I am cool and smart? How do I look, sitting here—hip and awesome, I hope? And I imagine that we are all doing that same thing, worried about what other people are thinking, and yet assuming that we are the only one.

I can't wait to catch up and actually get to talk to you in person. I know you, but I don't know anything about you. I don't even know your name or where you are from or what your favorite music is, or what kind of things make your heart beat faster. I look forward to learning all those things about you, and to times where we can be human with one another and not just inconveniences.

Those eyes of yours break my heart. The restless uncertainty. The darting back and forth. The despair. More so than anything else, I know that about you. That like so many of us, you are fundamentally dissatisfied and restless. A feeling that I know well—trust me. You put on a decent front, as do most people. But at the core you're just like everyone else—searching for something you just can't seem to find. Have you ever thought about that? We live in one of the richest countries in the world. Luxury, comfort, and mindless entertainment to keep you busy your entire life if you want. But so many people are exceedingly bored and miserable. Weary from a thousand trivial little boredoms. We've all become experts at diverting our dissatisfaction into entertainment and a thousand other places, but it's inescapable. We're like kids at Christmas, unwrapping gift after gift only to find coal inside the box. And then we look around with darting eyes for the next present, somehow believing that it will be different than the last. It's quite a desperate business.

I need to tell you something. Well, more than something—a story actually. You may not believe me, and that's okay. All I ask is that you hear me out. I can convince you of nothing. All I can do is tell you what I need to tell you.

I know you have no reason to trust me right now, and I can't properly explain why I care about you so much. But this I know: we are kindred spirits. The only way to understand is to keep reading.

I hope that maybe, just maybe, the next time I see you those darting eyes of yours will be still.

When this is over and we get to talk, I hope you will be honest with me. That we can at once cut through all the masks, the frivolity, and the endless surface-level bullshit of life. I hope somehow you remember what we shared, so that we can start there.

Nice to meet you, I guess, or talk to you, or whatever. I can be a bit awkward as you will presently see. But what is life without awkwardness? It's one of the things that make us human.

2

I'm not sure where to start.

Probably with Chloe.

Chloe.

How can I attempt the blasphemy of putting her on paper?

When Chloe and I were first married, I used to tiptoe into our room after she was asleep and kneel down beside the bed next to her. I would sit there for twenty, thirty minutes and just watch her sleep. I would watch her chest rise and fall, play with her brown hair falling off of the pillow. My favorite times were when her mouth would be cracked open, lying on her back. That's just funny, to see a person sleeping like that. She was just so adorable, so sweet and innocent, and it made my insides scream I was so enamored with her. I would bend down and kiss her on the cheek over and over, and it would make me feel so calm and at peace. Like nothing else mattered, and everything would be okay because this would never change. No matter what a day brought, I could enjoy the peace of watching my precious new bride sleep, and then crawl into a warm bed beside her.

Oh, Chloe. I would give anything to be able to watch her sleep tonight.

I heard a while back that there are over 17 million Americans that are clinically depressed. 17 million. Can you believe that? Pick any 18 people that you know, and odds are one of them is so bad off that a medical professional diagnoses them with a clinical illness—not counting the lesser throes so many have that are not "clinical" in nature. Wow. And if that number doesn't seem terribly high to you at this point, I think that is an even scarier indicator of where we are.

I've been thinking a lot about advertising lately. When it is boiled down, I think advertising can be summed up in two very simple steps. One—the advertiser sets out on his task to make you feel unhappy. You do not have this product. Your skin does not look like that. Your kitchen is incomplete because it doesn't have one of those. In other words, you are unhappy. Something is missing from your life. There is a gaping void in your soul, ravaging from unmet needs. Of course this is just playing on the already present existential malaise that we all feel. The hook can be anything—from a cheeseburger to a self-propelled vacuum cleaner to more toned abs.

And then comes step two—the attempt to convince you that if you just had this or that that I just happen to be selling, you would in fact be very happy. As happy as the person on TV was when they got theirs, if not more. There's a chance you could even have sexy women in bikinis hugging all over you while you eat that cheeseburger that's already making you happy, and of course that is just a cherry on top. Exponential happiness.

I heard that the average American sees three thousand advertisements a day. Three thousand. Is that true? At first, I didn't think so. And then I thought, maybe I'm just numb to so many of them already that I don't even notice them? Regardless, we won't argue over that statement, as if we could prove it anyway. You can count if you want. I'd be interested, though it seems an unbearably tedious task.

Let me know if you do, though.

So anyway, we see a lot of ads everyday. Thousands or however many. We are being told, thousands of times a day, "You are unhappy. You are unhappy. You are very, seriously, miserably unhappy." Whispered in our ears over and over, by commercial after billboard after commercial after billboard. Incessantly. What a troublesome and despairing business. No wonder so many people are depressed.

Our entire economic system is built on unhappiness.

Liars! All of them. As if you didn't already know from your constant need to return to the shady profiteers, to new and shinier models. Lies. Lies. Lies. You have been lied to. A lot. The self-help books that smile at you with their big white teeth from the shelf at Barnes and Noble? The cheery slogans and hunky dory platitudes? Liars! All the self-help books in the world will not fix you. "Try harder" and "do better" won't get you anywhere.

Don't be fooled. The voices that call you to their merchandise tables do not love you. They offer no hope and only want to make a buck off of your emptiness. If I know anything I know that; I believed the lies, too. And then I lied to Chloe.

I know you're reading this and what you may be thinking. But please hear me out. If it gets too personal, if you don't like what you are hearing, if you don't believe me—push through. And trust that I am only telling you what I'm telling you because I love you. Ask yourself, if I were another smiling face that patted you on the back and told you what you wanted to hear, would I really be loving you?

Now I've just got to get this thing written before you leave. But the good news is you look like you are settled in for a while. Don't hurry, friend. Give me some time, okay?

3

I can be the king of tangents, and you may not necessarily care about them—but I hope that one day we will be good enough friends that you won't mind listening to my tangents, though. Maybe one day.

So, about me: I'm 29 years old and work at *The State* newspaper as a columnist. You may have read some of my work before.

I have two twin boys, Liam and Isaac, who are 3 year-old tornadoes. They love to breakdance.

I grew up here in the Columbia area, but I went to Clemson for undergrad, and my blood runs orange. (Oh no. I hope you're not a South Carolina fan, but I guess we can still be friends if you are. I'll just have to take you to Clemson sometime. You'll convert.)

I hold the touchdown reception record at Lexington High School (18 my senior year). Yep, I'm that guy…lame enough that I still brag about high school sports even though I'm pushing 30.

I love thousand island dressing and will eat it on anything. Including scrambled eggs and spaghetti.

Okay, one more. This one is going somewhere, I promise. So I used to live in what I call "zombieland," which is where I think most Americans live. What I mean by that is when you are not really honest with anyone about anything, your relationships are half-ass and about as deep as a summer mud puddle. "How are you?…I'm fine, I'm fine…Boy the weather sure is nice today, isn't it?….Sure is Bob, sure is…" You know what I mean. I don't live in zombieland anymore, though. Because at the end of the day, what good does hiding it all do? Everyone knows we're all lying anyway. Sometimes when I am talking to someone I just want to shake them—"Enough of your bullshit…tell me how you are *really* doing."

Actually, forgive me. I just told you a lie, and that's not a great way to start off a friendship. What I mean by "I don't live in zombieland anymore" is that I don't live there maybe half the time. I am still stuck in those shadows all too often. But I am trying to get free. I am.

I hope you can join me.

4

I fear that you will not even have read this far, that you will have put the story down and therefore invalidated my existence with your indifference. I'm a writer, after all, and I'm afraid that this won't be interesting enough, or well-written enough, to merit your time. What can I say, approval is my drug of choice.

It's my dad's fault, really.

This scene plays in my mind, over and over. I'm six years old, and my dad is sitting in his recliner drinking a beer and watching TV like he always does. Johnny from down the street had shown me a karate move earlier that day, and I'm standing in front of him.

"Daddy, look! Look what I can do. Johnny taught me." I raise my hands in the air and do a chop/kick combo that seemed awfully cool at the time. He nods, takes another sip of beer, not looking at me for even a second. I try it a few more times and he stays glued to the TV, oblivious to me.

I don't remember what he looks like, or really anything about him at all. Just the feeling of being ignored. And the smell of it.

How much of what we do is just a six-year-old boy saying, "Look Daddy, look!" Anyone, anybody—look, notice me, pay attention, applaud, pat me on the back and tell me I'm worth something.

Maybe you know what I mean. I bet you do. Maybe someday you'll tell me about it.

Later that night, the night of my karate show, something happened.

But I need a refill. The Sumatra is especially good today.

5

Okay, I'm back. And you're still there, typing away on your computer now. Maybe you're writing a letter to me? That would be fun.

I hope you're not writing about how lonely you are. I was feeling kind of lonely earlier today. It's been one of those days full of thoughts and regrets, and I'm trying to grab them and process accordingly. But, it's a little overwhelming. I'm sure you can relate.

You know what would be awful? If all of us sitting here in this coffee shop three feet from each other were blazing away at our keyboards or journals, writing about how lonely we all feel. I've thought about that before. Wouldn't that be tragic?

So that night, my father left.

I'm lying there in my bed, tiny hands pressed so tight against each ear that I think I might crush my skull. I wish my hands were thicker, soundproof, impenetrable against the shrieking. I clutch Peter the panda against my chest with my elbow. I try not to hear. Desperately. Pillows. My closet. Humming. Nothing could drown out the fighting.

Useless hands.

They fight for a while, and I hear the door slam. Sara is screaming, so I tiptoe to her room and find Mom picking her up and rocking her back to sleep. Mom's eyes are tired and watery. I ask her where Daddy is and she says he's gone. I ask her when he is coming back, and she says never.

Never.

I had no idea what that meant.

I ask her if he left because of me. I had dropped the coffee pot that morning and it shattered all over the kitchen floor. My terrified gasp proved to not be uncalled for—he yelled and screamed and was pissed the rest of the day.

Mom looks me in the eye. "No, no, no, honey, not at all! Don't you dare think that, bud. Your dad left because, because of —" she stops herself, realizing that I probably won't understand. "Your dad loves you and I'm sure he'll be back to see you from time to time. Come here and sit with Mommy, sweetheart," she says. I climb up into her lap and put my head on her chest, right beside Sara's. I distinctly remember the sweet, innocent smell of her hair that night.

The next thing I remember, Mom's wiping tears from my face. She rocks and caresses my face, whispering over and over, "Shhh…shhh. Everything is gonna be okay."

I put forth a heroic effort to pull it together; blubbering is not exactly the best way to start your career as man of the house.

For a moment that night, I closed my eyes as tightly as possible and held the pose for a few seconds, almost pushing my eyeballs back into my brain. Then I opened them wide and looked toward the door, hoping like fire to see Daddy standing there in the doorway, coming to tell Mom to stop crying, because he was there and everything was okay. But the blurriness faded to an empty doorway. A little bit later I did it again. And again. And again.

He never came.

When I finally gave up, Mom was beginning to calm down and breathe deeply. She rocked still, her eyes shut and head tilted back. Sara sighed, and I looked over at her, bent down and kissed her on her forehead. Don't worry, baby sister, I thought. I'll take care of you.

What a miserable broken promise that turned out to be.

6

That was the last time my dad would grace our family with his presence, as you probably figured out. Another single mom, left to work herself to death because of a selfish and irresponsible man. You know the drill.

I'll shut up about that now. I'm dealing with it, I promise. And I know even people who had good dads have those same thoughts. We are all broken one way or another.

If you don't think you are, I will let life wake you up in good time. It tends to do that.

So, back to Chloe. There we were, a couple of months ago. The kids running around in the yard, Chloe double-checking the suitcases. I ran after the kids, catching Liam under my right arm and then going for Isaac in my left. "Come on, you little munchkins," I said, running with both of them tucked under each arm, sideways like tiny airplanes. We went straight to the car, where I put them both down and helped them in, buckling their car seats tight. My phone started buzzing in my pocket, but I silenced it and walked around to hug my wife. "Please be careful, honey. I love you."

"I love you too," she smiled, giving me a peck on the cheek. "I really wish you were going with us," she said, with that sad smile like she was giving me one more chance to acquiesce. "A week is a really long time to be away from you."

"Chloe, you know I would love to—but really, I just can't. The next few days at work are gonna be nuts. It's just bad timing."

"You can write from anywhere you know…they have this thing called the Internet."

"Honey, I'm sorry. You are going to have a great time with your parents, and you'll be back before we know it." My phone buzzed again.

"They're going to be mad at you for not coming, you know," she said.

"Won't be the last time."

"Who's calling you?"

"I don't know…probably someone from work about another deadline." I reached down and silenced it once again. I bent down and kissed her on the forehead. "Goodbye, sweetheart. Be careful and have fun. Tell them I said hello and I'm sorry for not being able to get away from work."

"I will," she said, getting in the car. The back windows were down, and I peeked in to tell the boys goodbye. "Bye boys, y'all take care of mommy, okay?"

"Hug! Hug! Hug!" They both screamed.

"Okay, okay," I said, opening the door and leaning in for Liam to wrap his tiny arms around my neck. He kissed me on the cheek. I walked around to the other side and did the same for Isaac, then closed the door and blew a kiss to them as they backed out of the driveway and started down the road.

My phone vibrated again, and I quickly reached in my pocket to grab it. The caller ID lit up—*Jordan.*

"Hello there," I answered playfully.

"Jack! You were supposed to be here at six. Where are you? I was getting worried."

"Just running a little bit late seeing them off, that's all."

"Okay, fair enough. But if you knew what was waiting for you you'd have left already."

"You cooked me dinner? How sweet of you!"

"You know I don't cook, Jack. But I am laying on my bed with a little lacy pink thing on."

"Even better," I said. "I'm getting in my car right now." I put my phone back in my pocket and walked over to my car.

Before I got to the end of the road, my phone rang again. It was Chloe.

"Hey Chloe, something wrong?"

"No—I just forgot to ask you to be sure to take out the trash tonight. It's getting piled up in the bin outside."

"Sure I will." I responded, heart rate increasing.

"Are you in your car? Where are you going?"

"Just out to get a bite to eat." Sometimes I even surprised myself how quickly the lies came to mind.

"Oh okay. Go get yourself something good since you are a bachelor this week. You're gonna need some energy for all that work you've got to do."

"Yeah, I think I will. I might get some Olive Garden to go, I've been craving chicken alfredo something serious."

"Mmm, that sounds good. That's where our last date was, wasn't it?"

"Yeah, I think you're right. It was."

"That was too long ago—we need to get away soon, just me and you. I miss you, Jack."

I thought about playing the joke that she had only been gone for two minutes, but it was clear she wasn't talking about that. "I miss you too, honey. Be careful, and text me when you get there tonight so I'll know you are okay."

"Okay. Bye, Jack." She hung up the phone. I swallowed deeply, evaded my conscience with the skill of a bullfighter, and lost myself in thoughts of Jordan in her lingerie for the rest of the drive.

I make myself sick.

7

One morning I woke up, I don't remember when it was—and the first thought that popped into my head was, is this it? Is this all there is to life? Four or five more decades of this? If I'm lucky my 401(k) will do well and maybe I'll get a boat, and then I'll die and rot? It was a maddening thought.

That's when I knew I had to find something. Anything. I think this happens to some people and they find a new hobby or a new career or just another beer. And I found Jordan. It's really that simple I think.

Have you ever had that thought? What a despairing, suffocating thing it is. It took over my life, essentially. It told me what to do. It told me Jordan's sparkling eyes just might be the cure-all for my despair.

I'm a deep thinker—always have been. It's stuff like this that really bothers me, or things that I just can't figure out. It tends to keep me up at night. Occasionally I take prescription sleeping pills to be able to sleep. Okay, maybe more than occasionally. Maybe every night. But the thing is, the thirty minutes between when I take my Ambien and when my head feels like a floating pool of motor oil are the worst. I'm not kidding, sometimes it feels almost unbearable. Side effects, I guess, though that is not on the warning label or the commercials.

"*Warning*: may make you think way too deeply about life than you are comfortable with. But don't worry, it will knock you out soon after."

I watch TV during that time to try to numb myself, but it never seems to work. One night I remember watching a special about the ancient Egyptians on the History channel. I watched the tombs and mummies being excavated, the archaeologists sweeping the dust around with their little brooms. Then, the thought: *Dust.* We are all going to be dust…me, my family, this house, everything. Then I curled up in a ball on my couch and waited for the heaviness to overwhelm me.

Then, there was the time that the Discovery channel got me in all kinds of a funk. I was trying to go to sleep when Planet Earth came on. Have you ever seen any of those? Incredible. It was probably a bad idea to watch it during one of my Ambien-induced throes, however.

So it comes on and I'm lying there watching these amazing shots of glaciers, barrier reefs, the Himalayas. Then—the damn whales. It was the whales that really got me. The massive, beautiful strides they take, sliding through the water effortlessly and making that noise that just might be able to put me to sleep without medication. And this horror came over me: What does this all mean? What is this crazy planet we all live on?

And then I thought about God. Thanks a lot, Ambien. I took another pill. And it made me late for work the next morning.

Do you ever think about the more meaningful questions of existence? I hope you aren't watching so much TV that you don't ever have to really think about anything. I heard the average American watches three hours of TV a day. I got curious a while back and added up what that means—twenty-one hours a week (obviously), over forty-four whole twenty-four hour days per year. Over an average seventy-year lifetime, 3,115 days would be spent doing nothing but watching TV.

That is eight and a half years of your life.

Yes, you heard that right. Seems like it might be wasting our lives. I don't really want to lie on my deathbed and think about all the great TV I watched, do you? If that is you, I don't mean to offend you. I'm just saying. Maybe you should go outside some. Spend time with friends. If you don't have many friends, make more. Read a book. I think you will be a happier person if your life doesn't just consist of eat, TV, sleep, work, eat, TV.

8

So the next morning after Chloe left to go to her parents, I pulled away from Jordan's condo to run home and shower before work. I was so sleepy that I stopped for a second longer at a stop sign to try to wake up enough to drive without killing somebody. As I did, I noticed a billboard with a familiar logo in the bottom right hand corner—it was a church that did a lot of advertising in the paper. Typically their ads featured their pastor sitting there with blinding white teeth, grinning like he just hit the lottery, and his wife standing there like she just walked out of the plastic surgeon's office.

But my eyes cleared and it wasn't. It was an ad that read in massive bold letters:

"CHRISTIANITY IS THE BEST THING FOR OUR BROKEN WORLD."

You probably have heard of this church. And you most likely know that they are anything but the best thing. More of a political country club for upper-middle class white people. I guess this was their definition of making a difference in the community, huh? Pathetic.

As I drove home I got an idea. "Yep. It's time." I said to myself. Settled. Done. My frustration morphed into a smile…I was going to have some fun with this.

I sped to work that morning and churned out a column about the billboard.

It was titled, "I Respectfully Disagree." I even got a picture of the billboard to put beside it. I opened it with, "Forgive me if I am unimpressed with the contributions Christians and churches have made to society over the past few years."

It was a pretty scathing indictment of Christianity, tackling the usual list of suspects: hypocrisy, judgment, lack of concern for the poor, televangelists, pastor scandals involving money, sex, or worse—child molestation. The Crusades. Slavery. And the fact that a lot of good-ole' southern church people fought to keep the rebel flag flying at our state house—a reality that not only consistently hurts a lot of people, but our economy as well.

It was pretty harsh, though I did go back and edit a few times to scale it down to what I thought was reasonable. I ended it with the popular Gandhi quote: "I like your Christ, but I do not like your Christians. Your Christians are so unlike your Christ."

Maybe you think it was too harsh of me. Or maybe you are right there in the boat with me and you have seen some ugly stuff. Trust me, nothing you have seen is as ugly as what I've seen.

9

One time I walked up to a guy named Ben, a Christian who works downstairs, and acted really sad. I asked him to pray for me and he perked up like he would rather do that than anything else in the world. He asked me what I needed prayer for. I told him that I believed I had been possessed by a demon the night before. I made up this elaborate story about how I was in my garage cleaning and listening to rock and roll, which I guess indeed is the devil's music, because this demon crawled out of the radio somehow and took control of my body. I rolled my eyes in the back of my head and started convulsing, to show him what it was like. He flipped. I couldn't keep it up, however, and started laughing. He huffed out of his cubicle. I'm not sure we've talked since then.

Would you like to hear about the time I got "saved"? I may as well be straightforward with you.

I was maybe ten years old, and Uncle Richard had dragged Sara and me to a revival service at his church because he was babysitting us that night so Mom could work. I despised the smell of that place, and even more so I detested Uncle Richard's stank breath that would shower us while we sang hymns we didn't know. Ladies in their frills and flowers would swoon over Richard, pinching our cheeks and all that rot.

He was a good deal older than Mom, but still single, or a "eunuch," as he called it. He was a big help for a single mom, he always said. He had a better job than Mom, working in sales at an office supply company, and he never seemed to do much outside of working and serving as a deacon at his church. As much as I hated this man, I'd be lying if I said he never put food on our table.

I tried to daydream as much as possible during the service, but the visiting preacher, with all his pomp and circumstance and angry diatribes and hellfire, made that difficult. His long, bony finger looked like a lightning bolt could jolt out of it at any second.

Near the end, he transitioned into what he called the invitation. He told everyone to bow their heads and close their eyes, and to raise their hand if they wanted to respond to his invitation, start behaving, and be saved. I didn't even realize my eyes were open, I don't think. I just sat there, eyelids glued back, taking in this moment that seemed some grown-up secret that kids weren't privy to.

"I see that hand, brother. Amen. Repent today" the preacher man said, then paused for a moment.

"Yes sister, I see that hand. And you too, brother, I see your hand. Glory to God…welcome to the kingdom of the beloved."

But no one was raising a hand. Not a single soul.

I stared wide-eyed at the preacher in a moment of bewilderment. Suddenly, the man's eyes met mine and I panicked like a thief caught in the very act. I had no idea what to do, so I quickly shut my eyes and put my head down. Very reverently, of course. My heart thumped the wall of my tiny chest.

But then he asked the boy in the blue shirt to come down front. I kept my head down and ignored it until Uncle Richard elbowed me in the side. I was the only boy in there, so you really didn't even need the blue shirt qualifier.

When I finally reached the front I thought I might pass out. I steadied my knees and stood tall as the preacher man knelt down eye level with me. "Do you understand your wickedness, son?" he said, loud enough for everyone to hear.

I nodded my head up and down, thinking it was most likely the correct answer.

"Do you want to repent of your unrighteousness and be saved from the demons of hell?"

I nodded once more, then looked over my shoulder at Uncle Richard, who wore a dumb, approving smile plastered on his face. I didn't want to do anything to make him smile. When I turned back to face the preacher man, he stared into my eyes with the ferocity of a pissed off cat. He was close enough now for me to feel his wet breath on the top of my nose. His sweat smelled like fried okra and made me want to puke.

"Wonderful, then," he said, standing up again and shifting his eyes away from mine slowly. He put his hand firmly around the back of my neck and presented me to the congregation.

"Join me as I pray over this lad's soul," the preacher said, proceeding into a quality-sounding prayer like something you hear on TV. And just like that, I was saved. From what, I wasn't sure.

After the prayer I trekked back to my pew, avoiding the stares and smiles pointed at me. Uncle Richard put his arm around me as the congregation stood to sing. The only lines of that hymn that stuck in my mind are, "washed in the blood of Jesus."

Only, I didn't feel washed.

In fact, I felt dirtier than ever.

10

So yeah, that should give you an idea of what my experience with Christianity was like. My mom was unintentionally unreligious while we were growing up, so the only tastes I got were from my uncle.

I still get a queasy feeling in my stomach when I see his name. Has this ever happened to you? You see something or hear something and it makes a connection in your mind somehow, and this memory or image comes to mind of something that happened to you in the past, and for a moment you really believe that it didn't really happen to you. It was someone else, it is a scene from a bad movie or something, but it didn't really happen to you. Then, you see the picture again and realize the little boy or little girl, or teenager or adult in the scene is you and the horror that you had forgotten punches you in the stomach? Repression, they call it. I think that word doesn't do the feeling justice. It should be a much nastier word that feels more grotesque and weighty. It should sound harsh and throat-punchy.

I hope you don't have anything that you need to repress. I really, really do. I hope there is nothing but smiles in the deepest memory banks you have.

You may have guessed this already, but I have to tell you, I think. I hope I can trust you. I hope this has never happened to you.

I don't forget that this really happened to me. But at the same time, I do. Does that make sense?

A while back I was walking through the kids section at Barnes and Noble, looking for something for Liam and Isaac. I walked past an old-school book about Barbie, and in an instant this scene in my memory unlocked and unleashed its fury on me.

I'm sitting on the floor in Uncle Richard's house one night, maybe eight or nine years old, watching some cartoon on TV. I'm oblivious to the world, but shaken out of the stupor by Sara screaming. I get up and run down the hall, pushing open Uncle Richard's bedroom door. Sara is lying across the foot of his bed, naked, Uncle Richard standing over her, fumbling with his pants.

That piece of shit.

I yelled, "What are you doing to her?" and ran over and swung at him as hard as I could. He caught my fist in motion and squeezed it, twisted my arm behind my back until I screamed.

I made eye contact with Sara, her head cocked over to the side, blonde curls hanging off the bed. The wildness in her eyes petrified me. I lashed out one more time, threatened to tell Mom about what he was doing. I didn't fully know what was happening, I don't think, but it felt like the most wrong thing I could imagine at the time.

He bent down and put his hand around my throat, starting to squeeze. "You tell your mom anything about this—I will hurt your sister very badly. You hear me?" I couldn't breathe at all, much less shake my head. "Remember what your mom told you, God wants you to obey your elders." With that, he let go of me and I choked on oxygen. "Now take your clothes off, Jack." He then held up two dolls—a Barbie and a Ken, both without clothes, and said something about a game we were going to play.

Shit…I'm about to cry. I'm sorry, I need to go for now. I need a beer.

11

Okay. I'm back. Sorry about that. I got some fresh air and then got a Guinness. Isn't it awesome that Immac sells beer as well as coffee? I wish every coffee shop did. Sometimes you just need both, you know?

It sucks that typically in life we forget the things we want to remember, but remember the things we want to forget.

Isn't it crazy how our scars stay with us? I mean, I would think that after so many years I would be able to put that stuff behind me for good. But even now if it hits me at the right time it can land me in the fetal position. What gets me the most is thinking about Sara. That precious, sweet little girl. And the truckload of issues she has now because of *him*.

I was talking with someone a while back who is in his fifties. He was telling me about how badly he was teased when he was in middle school and high school. Sissy, faggot, they called him. He said to this day when he hears those words he cringes and he can feel the same pain as he did back then. He had a high school reunion a while back and the day of, he decided that he couldn't go. He was afraid to be there because of three guys that were the worst bullies, who were so mean to him that he couldn't even talk about it. Can you believe that? He stayed home from his high school reunion because he couldn't stand to face people that he hadn't seen in decades.

A few weeks later, he ran into one of the guys in a grocery store. The guy was nice and acted like they were just long lost friends, like he was so happy to have run into him. My friend told me the only thing he could think was, "Do you not remember everything you did to me?"

It really is crazy how much damage we human beings can inflict on one another.

I mean really, being human is a tough thing to figure out. I know that. One big predicament—the human predicament, I call it. But, you would think that if figuring out life was so difficult, then all of us humans would kind of be on the same team, you know? We would be looking out for one another and trying to support each other. Or at least staying out of each other's way.

But—have you ever thought about the fact that when you come home at night you lock the door? Why do you do that? You are not keeping a raccoon from coming in and shitting on your living room floor. You are keeping other people out. Other humans, who are in this giant predicament right beside you.

I would venture to say that like me, the greatest wounds you have by far have come from other people. People that you loved, admired, cherished and respected, and maybe still do. But they have hurt you the worst. It's like we all carry around these little knives and we are constantly cutting each other, and occasionally we just stab one in really, really deep.

I don't want you to think that my life was nothing but this awful string of memories like the ones I've shared. Don't worry, my life is not one of those stories that just gets worse and worse until it's almost unbelievable that all of that happened to one human being. Those stories do happen—I know people with them. But I am not one of them.

I have so many happy memories from growing up that I could not begin to put them on paper. Mom, Sara and I were a tight family and Mom did everything she could to fill in the gap left by an absent father. Single moms are saints in my book, hands down. One time she even dressed up like Santa Claus late one Christmas Eve and totally tricked us.

When I was a teenager, she needed to teach me how to shave, so she put shaving cream all over her face, laughing the whole time, and used the back of a plastic razor to pretend shave her face and show me how. That was classic Mom.

I didn't know this until much later, but she sold every piece of jewelry she had to pay for me to play Little League.

12

So there was a bit of an uproar about my column, but honestly not as much as I'd thought. I guess all the Christians took my warning seriously and put on their nice faces. I think that some people started a "Pray for Jack Bennett" Facebook group, which made me laugh. Hey, I'll take any prayers I can get, you know?

I was driving my usual late Sunday morning route to the coffee shop—it's my routine time every week to go relax while Chloe watches the kids. It was pouring rain and I was beyond frustrated because my windshield wiper blades were dried out and making that incredibly annoying squeaky sound. It has always made me cringe—that same sound of balloons being rubbed or styrofoam egg cartons. Ugh, I hate it. I tried turning them off, to see if I could see through the torrent. No such luck. Being annoyed is better than being dead.

I passed what I call *the* church on my way every week. What I mean by *the* church is the small little church that always has the most memorable sayings on their marquis. Some of them were hilarious, in a sad sort of way.

On Mother's Day: *Shock Your Mom—Come To Church*. That one may be my all-time favorite.

Don't Worry—Our Church Is Prayer Conditioned.

Party In Hell Cancelled Due To Fire.

Repent Now: Avoid The Rush On Judgment Day.

Want To Be Friends With Jesus, Angels And Saints? Try "Faith Book!"

You Have To Wonder About Humans. They Think God Is Dead And Elvis Is Alive!

Google Doesn't Have All Of The Answers.

Yikes. What a clever bunch. And apparently they've never been on Google.

You may not even believe this next part. That's fine. I don't believe it either.

I was hoping for a funny one that week. So when the letters became visible through the rain, I read the message aloud to myself:

What If Jack Is Right About Us?

I wasn't sure what I'd seen at first. I pulled into the church driveway to make sure I wasn't seeing things. I looked over, past the twenty or so cars in the parking lot toward the glowing stained-glass windows protruding from the grey morning, squinting through the rain towards the sign. But from the parking lot, it was hard to see.

And that's when I saw him.

A man, standing there, knocking on the door of the church.

And the door was not opening.

I turned the car off and sat for a second, watching the poor man in horror—the sign suddenly far from my mind. From the back he looked like a typical middle-aged white man you'd see at the library downtown, most likely homeless, but you couldn't tell for sure. He had on a blue Piggly Wiggly shirt, tattered blue jeans, and a dirty green backpack slung over one shoulder. His graying brown hair was pulled back into a ponytail. And he was standing there underneath the awning, calmly, gently knocking on the door.

So I got out of the car.

What else could I do?

My left foot splashed in a puddle on the way, soaking my shoe. I tried to shake the water off and made my way to the steps. I couldn't bring myself to run through the rain—I guess it was just too unusual of a situation for hurrying.

So I walked up the stairs, my hair dripping morning rain onto shoulders.

Knock, knock, knock, I heard as I reached the top step and the shelter of the awning above. I was standing twenty feet behind the man, who was still clueless to my presence.

Knock, knock. The man put his head down. I swallowed the awkward lump in my throat and shuffled my feet a little on the thin carpet, hoping he'd hear me and turn around. He didn't.

"Hello there," I finally mustered, when I could take it no longer.

13

He turns, not quickly, no—I may even say he turns quite confidently for a man in his predicament. The first thing I notice about him is his eyes. They are—how can I describe them? Not noticeably beautiful or colored, but penetrating. Yes, penetrating, that's the word. Big, brown, piercing eyes that seem to hold your gaze for longer than is customary. The rest of his weathered face reveals little, but his eyes own a peaceful, slow gaze over me, and to my surprise, he didn't seem very embarrassed at all. It had been a while since I'd gone down to the shelter to serve—more than a while if I'm honest—and I guess I'd forgotten how being homeless could steal the last trace of dignity from a soul.

"Hello," he responds, his beard cracking with a smile.

He confused me, to be honest. So many of these fellows, you know, have that look about them—that frightened, untrusting, frantic look that seems to cloud every facet of their interaction with others. But this man, though nowhere near as advanced in years, made you feel like you were meeting your grandpa for coffee. He just had that air about him.

He made no rush to say anything else, so I ventured out with the first thing that popped in my head. "Maybe they didn't hear you?" I tried to rope it in towards the end of the sentence, to change it to something less, well, stupid, but it was to no avail. I was cursed with a quick tongue.

"Oh no, they heard me all right." He answered. "A nice gentleman escorted me out here and told me to come back when I was more presentable. I started knocking, and they just started singing louder when I didn't stop."

I leaned over toward the door and caught the wave of voices. There was a crescendo of music, and then the chorus:

I have decided, to follow Jesus.
I have decided, to follow Jesus.
I have decided, to follow Jesus.
No turning back, no turning back.
Though none go with me, I still will follow…

They continued and I turned back to the man. I remembered the song from way back when, and my heart burned with fury at these imbeciles and with compassion for my new friend. The man still stood silently, smiling like a kid who just got left out of dodge ball but didn't want to let on that his feelings were hurt.

"Don't worry about these morons," I said as reassuringly as possible. He looked down at his feet. "Hey, are you hungry?" I asked. "Would you be up for some coffee and a bagel?"

"Yes, I think I would like that, thank you very much." He answered. "It's been a while since I've had a good meal, and some hot coffee would hit the spot."

"Perfect." I said, glad to be able to take him away from his misery here. Before turning to walk, I gave the locked double door a swift kick for good measure, and the frame rattled and shook. I'd like to think it scared the bejeezus out of at least one person.

We jogged through the rain and jumped into my Range Rover. "Sorry about getting the seat wet," he remarked, fingering the leather after closing the passenger side door.

"No problem…it won't hurt them at all." I lied. I had just bought the car—used, but still. I was cringing on the inside.

"I'm not interrupting anything, am I?" he asked.

"No…" I answered. "I was just headed to get some breakfast myself, and I've got plenty of time. No rush."

"Okay, good."

"A bagel sounds delicious right about now," I said as I pulled out of the church parking lot and onto the main road, trying to reassure him that he was no bother. "I'm glad I ran into you this morning—" I stopped as I realized the extent of my rudeness. "I'm sorry, sir, I never asked your name."

"Well, my friends call me Yeshua. So you can call me that since you just got me out of this weather…"

"Yeshua," I repeated. "That's an unusual name. I like it. Nice to officially meet you, Yeshua. My name is Jack. It's a pleasure."

"The pleasure is all mine," he responded, giving me a firm shake. "Thanks for picking me up." He smiled like he was really glad to see me, but I guess anyone would be happy to get out of that situation.

And if you think you know where this is going, just wait.

14

We went to Cool Beans (because Immac is closed on Sundays), ordered a couple of bacon egg and cheese on everythings, and sat down at a table in the corner, glad to be out of the weather. The rain fell cautiously down the window behind my new friend's back, and he began to eat like he hadn't in a while.

"Mmm...mmm." He said, after a few bites. "Delicious."

"Indeed," I responded, finishing a sip of coffee. I hesitated to talk much because I wanted to let him eat and enjoy his warm coffee. The awkward silence ended up getting the best of me though, as it typically does. "So, Yeshua, what's your story?"

His eyes gleamed a bit and he raised his head, pondering the question. "What's my story?" he said. "Well, that depends on how much time you have."

"Oh, I'm all ears," I responded, but also glanced down at my watch to politely let him know that I did not want to spend all day here.

He got the clue, and responded by smiling and not launching into his life story, sipping his coffee like it was getting lukewarm too fast. I felt bad, so I said the first thing that came to my mind. "So, what brought you to the church this morning? I guess that's the first time you've ever been locked out of a church, huh?"

He chuckled. "No, I wish. To be truthful, I've been locked out of a fair share of churches in my day." I gave him a confused squint, but kept silent. He cleared his throat and went on.

"Did you read that column in last week's paper?"

"The column about Christianity?"

"Yes, that one."

"Actually, I wrote it."

"You did? Wow. So you're Jack Bennett, huh? The man, the myth, the legend…"

"Ha, funny—yeah, that's me."

"I've been reading your column for a long time. You're a good writer. You've gotten into some interesting territory with this column I bet. Were you out driving around just in case picketers came to your house?"

"Ha. No, not really. I doubt that will happen. I hope not, at least."

"You never know," he said, grinning.

"So what did you think of the column? I assume you're a Christian, even though the church you were at this morning just proves my point."

"Yes, you are right about that—that particular church is nothing but arrows in your bag. Unfortunately, I think you are right about a good bit of stuff in the column." He paused for a moment, letting that sink in as he sipped his coffee. "However, I also think you have a lot to learn."

"Is that right?" I responded, playing along. "And who is going to teach me what I've got to learn?"

He paused for a moment, as if my rhetorical question hadn't been rhetorical. "Well, I could, if you're willing to learn anything from a guy in my situation." He winked at me, and I didn't really know how to respond.

He went on, "What about breakfast here every Sunday morning, around this time? Next time will be my treat."

I thought for a moment, and felt a little guilty about how long it had really been since I'd done anything to help anyone who didn't have it as good as me.

"Sure, I could do that," I answered.

"But, you know, if your faith is important to you, I don't want to keep you out of church…" I gave a dramatic pause, then went on. "Oh, wait a minute, never mind—it's your fellow believers who are doing that." I hoped it wouldn't be too much—he seemed to have a good sense of humor.

"Touché, my friend, touché. Well, you just don't worry about that. And watch out or you and I might be having church right here in the coffee shop." I laughed at that, glad that he wasn't mad at my joke. His laugh was deep and throaty, one where you just wanted to keep making the person laugh to hear it.

He looked around at the other people at Cool Beans and got fidgety. "Well, Mr. Jack Bennett, local celebrity writer, I don't need to take up more of your time today. But I'll see you next week. Don't leave me hanging—I'd hate to waste a perfectly good bacon egg and cheese on everything."

"Okay, I won't. Nice to meet you." He got up and pushed his chair under the table, leaning over it.

"Oh, one more thing, Jack?"

"Yeah?"

"I'd like you to do something for me this week."

"Okay," I said, a bit surprised at his boldness. "What is it?"

"Repent of cheating on your wife and beg for her forgiveness. She is the best thing you have going for you and trust me, you don't need to screw it up anymore than you already have."

From the word 'repent,' that was the longest breathless period of my life.

"And if you don't expose the affair, I will."

I turned blue as he walked toward the door, then shouted back over his shoulder, "Thanks for the bagel," as he slipped out.

My stomach did a cartwheel and pushed all the buttons that make you want to puke.

15

After I recovered my breath, I ran out of the coffee shop and down the street for probably half a mile looking for him. All I found was a pile of spit on the ground from being doubled over, out of breath. So I turned around and went back to the coffee shop to clear my head.

I don't remember if you were there that morning. Maybe you go to Cool Beans on Sundays too? Maybe you remember seeing us there. That would be crazy if so.

I sat there for over an hour. Stunned, to put it lightly. I was reeling. My phone rang off the hook, but I just let it buzz in my pocket without even looking. My coffee went from lukewarm to nasty.

Who was this guy and how did he know about Jordan—or Chloe? Or anything? I had been *careful*—so very careful. I was impressed by my own ability to hide it, to be honest. My mind raced through all possible options, trying to figure out who knew, who could have told a complete stranger, and why. Regardless, he was going to get a lot more than he bargained for next week at the coffee shop. That is, if I didn't find him before then.

My phone finally got my attention.

"Jack! Where have you been? I've been calling for an hour!"

"Chloe, I'm sorry. I'm still at the coffee shop. Didn't hear my phone."

"Eight times? Isaac is throwing up—can you get home soon and help me?"

"Yes—I'm sorry. I need to finish up writing these few last paragraphs and I'll be there." What I really needed was time to go talk to Jordan.

"Working on a Sunday?"

"I know babe. I will be there in a little while, okay?"

"Okay. Come home soon. I could use your help."

Jordan had been beeping in the whole conversation.

"Hey sugar," I answered.

"Jack?"

I panicked—it sounded like it was still Chloe.

"Jack, are you there?" It was Jordan.

"Yeah, I'm here. Sorry bout that."

"Where are you? I've been calling you like crazy."

"I was on my way to your house and I got held up…sorry. I'll be there in a few minutes." Okay, so lately my Sunday morning coffee shop trips had included swinging by Jordan's place. I guess I forgot to mention that.

I swung by the church, by the way, now that the rain had stopped. The sign didn't have my little message on it anymore.

When I arrived at Jordan's, she had cooked breakfast for me, which was cold by now, of course. She looked rather disappointed. "Sorry," I said. "That looks great…will you warm my plate up? I'm starving." She rolled her eyes, knowing I was lying. It was 11:30. But it was the first time she had ever cooked for me, so she warmed it up and I started eating. She made small talk while I stuffed down the bites. I mainly just nodded to keep her talking and stayed lost in my thoughts.

"Jordan, we need to talk." I said, interrupting one of her stories about her morning.

"Okay…shoot," she said, a bit nervous.

"Have you told anyone about us?"

"No…" she answered, squinting her eyes at me. "Why do you ask?"

"Are you sure?" I said, with a bit of tone.

"Yes, I'm sure. I'm not an idiot. Why, does someone know? Did Chloe find out?"

"No, not her. But someone knows."

"How do you know?"

"It's not important—don't worry about it. I'll take care of it."

She looked like she was getting angry. "Jack, you know people are going to find out sooner or later. Isn't it about time we prepared for that?"

I sighed and turned away from her. "You know I'm not ready for that." I took a deep breath. "In fact, we need to take a break."

She recoiled and scowled at me. "What? What are you talking about? What about our plans?"

"I'm not saying they won't happen in the future. I'm just saying they aren't going to happen right now. I just need some time to think and clear my head."

She shook her head, said she knew I was going to do this to her and called me a few choice names.

"Jordan, it's not like that," I said. "I haven't changed the way I feel about you, and I would still love to end up being with you. But I just can't do this right now, okay? You understand I'm in a difficult spot here?"

"I understand that you like to do what you want to and you don't care who it hurts. That's what I understand." Tears started to fall at this point. "Will you please leave?"

I gave her a look that she didn't return, so I grabbed my keys off of the table and walked out the door.

16

My mom used to say something that drove me crazy—something
to the effect of "You can do whatever you want, but you will always be found out somehow." It seemed so trivial when we were
talking about cheating on a test or copying homework.

I stewed for a couple days, nervous the entire time that this
guy was actually going to tell Chloe somehow. Every time I saw her
I panicked, thinking that she might know. At first I wasn't going to
tell her, and I would have told you to get off my back if you
wanted me to. I was going to figure out how turn the tables on this
guy. But the reality of the situation kept hounding me until I
thought I was going to die.

So I decided I had to tell her.

After putting the boys to bed, Chloe tiptoed into the bedroom and closed the door behind her. "Are they asleep?" I asked,
reclining on the bed, face stuck in a book that I wasn't reading.

"Yes, I think so." She smiled, walked over and gave me a kiss
on the forehead. I know. I don't deserve her. "So, you gotten any
more flack about the column from last week?" It was the first
chance we'd had to talk in a while. To be honest, it caught me off
guard because I had completely forgotten about that silly column.

"A little bit—not much. People are funny. I told you about
the Facebook group, right?"

"Yes. Hilarious." She said.

"It was a little bold, but I'm glad I published it."

"You, bold? Nah."

"You've got me pegged, babe."

"I've had you pegged for a long time," she answered, winking at me with that smirk that made me fall for her so long ago. My resistance started fading with that smirk. She stood there, her back to me, nightgown flowing as she reached to put up her clothes. I suddenly felt like I was breathing a heavy, rotten steam and I blurted out, "Chloe, I've been having an affair."

"What did you say?" She turned and faced me on a dime.

There was no going back. "I'm so sorry, honey. I've been cheating on you with Jordan, a girl at work, for several months now. I have broken things off with her. I hope you can forgive me, I'll do anything to fix this." My tone was cold and almost emotionless. Contrite? No. Sorry for getting caught? Yes.

She looked straight through me with a totally blank stare, like she had just found herself in a nightmare. For some time, she said nothing, only stared. Then, she dropped to her knees, slowly bent over with arms hugging her stomach, and wept.

I sat there on the bed, motionless, watching my wife heave and sob. I wished for anything but that. Kicking. Screaming. Biting. Punching. Anything but that broken pile of despair on the floor. My heart swelled up with love for her and really for the first time, a sickening knot in my stomach tightened.

After a few minutes, I felt like I had to do something. So I made the decision to walk over to her, kneel down beside her, and put my hand on her back.

That was a mistake, if you didn't know so already.

She recoiled the second my hand touched her with a mighty backhand slap right across my left cheek. "Don't touch me!"

I knelt there in shock, face stinging, almost frightened by the vivid rage in her eyes. Then she went off:

"How could you do this, Jack? *Work?* Work is busy, huh? You stayed home from a family vacation so you could be with another woman? What a narcissistic son of a bitch you are!"

She stepped toward me and started punching me as hard as she could. I tensed up and took it. I don't want to try to remember all of the other things she called me.

Finally, she stopped punching me and screamed, "Get out! Pack your bags and get out of my house. Now!" My male ego wanted to kick in right then. She knew good and well that I paid for the house and most of everything we owned. She hadn't worked since before the boys were born. But thankfully, before my mouth opened I remembered that this was no time for ego or anything related. So I grabbed a few changes of clothes and stuck them in a suitcase, snagged my toothbrush and a toiletry bag from the bathroom, and walked past her.

I stopped at the door, turned to her, and said, "I really am sorry, honey."

"Don't call me *honey*," she answered, calmed a little more now. "And get out of my house."

A few minutes later, I pulled up at the Extended Stay Motel, glad to see that the vacancy light was on. A very hairy man named Bill welcomed me to my new abode. I checked into my room, and then my phone buzzed. It was a text from Chloe:

Like father like son, I guess. Your mother would be sick. Pathetic.

I'm afraid I do not have sufficient words to portray my outburst of anger at that. Let's just say I had to replace a few things in the hotel room and leave it at that. She knew—she knew how much I hated my dad and what he did to my family. I called her about ten times to scream at her, but of course she didn't answer. When I calmed down, I replied to her text:

I'll tell you what's pathetic—making love to you.

Then I grabbed my car keys and walked out the door to drive to Jordan's.

I can really be a prick sometimes.

17

Do you hate me now? You should. By all means, you should. Run over me with your hate train if you want. I'll take it.

Jordan wouldn't let me come in that night, by the way—she was still mad at me. But I definitely went there.

My dad. Had I turned into my dad? That thought haunted me like my own personal ghost for the next few days. I would lay in my hotel bed at night and watch the ceiling fan spin, beer in hand, and go back and forth between *My worst nightmare is true*, and *No way—I may have found someone else to be with, but I would never leave my boys like my dad did*.

For the most part, I landed on number two. Conveniently.

Speaking of my dad—here is the extent of what I knew of him growing up.

I remember asking about him a few times when I was really young, and Mom mostly just shrugged it off and changed the subject, or gave me some half answer that didn't explain anything. Then, when I was thirteen I believe, my curiosity got the best of me one day. I walked into our kitchen: "Mom, do you know where dad is now, or what he is doing? Just curious."

She turned back to me and dried her hands on a towel. She frowned and put her hands on my shoulders. "Honey, I am sorry but your father died. He had a heart attack last year. His sister called to tell me, but I just didn't want to bring it up with you two. I'm sorry."

And that was it.

So a few nights later, I'm lying in the hotel room one of those nights by myself, and I get this mad urge to talk to someone. I'm not really sure even about what—just to talk and know that someone else was there. I pick up my phone and have this terrible revelation—there is no one I thought I could call. No one. No family. No friends. No one.

I feel like a decent measure of the meaningfulness of life is how many people would come to my funeral if I died. Right then I felt like my number would have been zero. It's been low before, but not that low.

Ugh. Has that ever happened to you? I hope not. There is nothing lonelier than an empty hotel room and a cell phone mocking your plight.

I guess I should tell you more about Sara and what happened with Uncle Richard. I hesitate to tell you now, because I don't want you to think I'm playing some sad fiddle, trying to make you feel sorry for me after I just said maybe the meanest, stupidest thing possible to my wife. I promise I am not—I would do anything to take that back. Anything. This is just what is coming to my mind, so I guess I should tell you.

I told you about the first time it happened, which was in its own horrific way the worst. But honestly, as far as effect goes, I think the last time may have been the worst—at least for Sara.

It was only about a year since the first time, and he had just gotten through doing something to Sara that I won't put you through. Then, after he had done what he wanted, he got this sick look on his face, like a disgruntled customer. He huffed, zipped his pants up, and half-yelled, "You know what—I am finished with this." He looked straight at Sara. "You are nothing but damaged goods now."

And that was it. He never touched us again.

Damaged goods. Can you imagine someone saying that to a precious little girl? I think those were the two most important words she ever heard, the words that had the greatest effect on her.

Well, I guess I have to tell you this too now—the story of the only fight I have ever been in.

I was a junior in high school, walking into the football locker room. One of the guys on the team, AJ, was dating Sara at the time. Right when I walked into the door, I saw a group of guys standing at the back, AJ one of them, with his back to me. All I hear is Sara's name, and he bends over and starts making humping motions. All the guys laugh with that asinine high school immaturity, and I hear this other guy, Cam, say, "Why would you want to do that—that girl is *damaged goods*." Right about that time I came up behind AJ and everyone sucked all the air out of the room. Faces went blistery white. Cam was still in the process of turning around to see what the commotion was, but I didn't let him get turned around before I punched him so hard in the back of the head I thought my fist had shattered. He lunged forward and dented in a locker with his forehead, and I moved on to AJ while the rest of the cowards fled. I won the fight—or fights—if you are curious. I would probably call it a no-contest. Cam ended up in the hospital for two days, and I was awarded with a week suspension from school. Best involuntary vacation I've ever had.

18

Uncle Richard never touched us again, well—he didn't have any more chances to. A short while after that day, we were riding somewhere in the car with Mom, and I only remember the question that started it. Sara looks up at Mom and asks, "Mom, what does *damaged goods* mean?"

It all gets fuzzy after that. Mom asked more questions and Sara accidentally said something about Uncle Richard and everything fell into place for Mom. I remember her tears—so many tears. Sara crying because she realized what she had done—us both scared to death of what was going to happen now when he found out. Then her statement: "Don't worry, you guys—I promise you will never see him again."

She had no idea how right she was.

About three days later, the phone call came. Police had not even had time to start prosecuting the case yet, and Uncle Richard had been murdered in cold blood in his own home. His house was ransacked, and evidently he fought back against the robbery and got shot between the eyes. I kid you not.

Now before you go thinking that my mom had something to do with this—that is ridiculous. She could never do something like that. Plus, I remember the look on her face when she answered the phone. I don't think waking up on the moon would have surprised her more.

What did I think about it all? At first, I was just delighted. I began to think that maybe there was some kind of balance or

46

justice in the world after all, and felt an infinite relief that he was no longer alive. The last I had heard, they didn't know who had done it, and frankly I didn't care to know. I kind of imagined that God did it, and was thankful for the gesture. No one ever spoke about it in our family again. No funeral—no nothing. It was like a nightmare that just disappeared into the morning sun.

However, as time went on, my young logic introduced a new question that would worm its way into the bottom of my brain. It went like this: *Sara says something…the abuse stops…Uncle Richard dies.* What if I would have said something after the first time? Would it have saved that year of torture?

I know, I know. I was just a kid and I can't play that game. It wasn't my fault, blah blah. But, *knowing* it isn't true doesn't keep me from *believing* it. I was a coward. A failure. I had completely let my baby sister down in the only thing that would really ever matter. Every time I look into Sara's eyes it reminds me of that feeling.

So I don't look into her eyes much.

On more than one occasion, I have found myself thinking about Uncle Richard traipsing through some fiery pock-marked landscape with flames tickling his feet. It helps—but then again it really doesn't. So I just try not to think about him. Ever. Sometimes it works.

Okay. I'm really glad I get to stop writing about him now. You know everything. At least, up to this point.

19

Okay. I'm a little sick of writing about serious stuff right now. And I'm feeling a bit tipsy from that Guinness. I didn't eat lunch because I've got to keep writing this thing so I can finish before you leave. I have to give this to you *today*. And I'm quite the lightweight when I don't have food in my stomach.

If we can take a small break for a little foray into non-serious land I'd be much obliged.

Ugh. Loud guy just walked in. I know you notice him too. The guy on his phone that thinks his conversation is so important everyone in the joint needs to hear it. I can't stand people like that. People who have either have no idea how loud they are or just don't care. So annoying. Let's join together and start a campaign to start telling every unreasonably loud person we see how annoying they are.

So, speaking of loud guy, other things that piss me off:

Advertising. I've already mentioned this, I know. But you can't do anything these days without someone screaming their product at you. You can't drive down the road or even watch a YouTube video in peace. You can't even check your email without getting specific advertisements right there beside your mail.

By the way, that really freaks me out. The Internet is watching us.

It won't be long until you won't be able to go to the bathroom somewhere without someone grabbing you and going, "You are free to use that urinal right after this quick word from our

48

sponsor…" Wait, I forgot. Some urinals in public restrooms already have ads on those little things that make it smell better. It's official—you can't even pee without getting advertised to. Congrats, America!

Another one? Websites with automatic music playing that you can't figure out how to turn off. I hate that so much that I will immediately leave.

Oh, I know. This is another big one. People that use ALL CAPS ALL THE DAMN TIME. LIKE IN EMAILS. AND ON FACEBOOK OR TWITTER. DON'T PEOPLE REALIZE IT'S NOT FUN TO BE YELLED AT ALL THE TIME? IT'S ANNOYING AND IT STRESSES ME OUT. AND ALSO, IF EVERYTHING YOU SAY IS IMPORTANT OR ALL CAPS-WORTHY THEN *NOTHING REALLY IS.*

I do have one friend from college who is able to somehow pull it off—to use all caps at times and it is funny and not annoying. Her name is Kathryn. I don't know how she does it but I'll ask her sometime and let you know if you're interested. It's an art, I guess. Maybe she'll write a book about it sometime.

Okay, I'm really serious about this one. I hate—and I mean hate—when I hear people incessantly yap about how much they hate living in Columbia and how awful it is. Like those people sometimes in the Rant & Rave section of the *Free Times.* (I hope you read that, it's often very funny.)

Some people just need to get a life. I mean, I know this isn't the greatest place in the world to live. I know it's ridiculously hot and humid here. *Famously Hot,* even. (Speaking of things I hate, that slogan certainly makes the list.) And I know there are some really cool cities nearby that sometimes make you jealous.

But people—you live here! By choice or necessity, it doesn't matter. You are here. I just want to get you all together in a room and scream at you. Your griping and moaning is not doing anything to actually make the place better. So either a) shut up your groaning and start contributing to make it a better place to live or b) leave. See ya. Don't let the door hit you. Seriously—I'll buy you a Greyhound ticket if you need it. Ugh…

I'm really not drunk, I promise. The alcohol is affecting me a tad for sure, but I'm not drunk. I would never get drunk off of one beer.

You may have guessed this already, but I can be a silly drunk or an emotional drunk. But hey, that's better than being an angry drunk, you know? Today I would be mostly silly, but if I kept drinking I could go emo any second. Especially since I am listening to Dashboard. Dashboard Confessional, that is, in case you are unfortunately uninformed. Very unfortunately uninformed. And get off me if you are a hater. They are so good and I've loved them since college.

By the way, I see that you have a Mac, so I have a confession. I kind of look down on people who still use a PC and not a Mac. I understand if people can't afford one and opt for a PC, but when I talk to people who really do think that PC's are better, or see those commercials, I just kind of get this smirk on my face and I think, that's cute…that's really cute that you actually still think that.

But don't worry, I'm not a snob about anything else besides that. I promise.

I just emailed in a rant to the Free Times that said this:

Attention: this is a rant to all previous ranters ranting about how awful Columbia is and how much they hate living here. Please, for the love of everything good and holy in the world—shut up. Quit your bitching and moaning and start actually contributing something to make our city better. Or, you could just leave. Move to a cooler city and find other snooty people with corncobs up their derrieres to sit around and be snobs with. That's all. Thanks for your precious time.

20

Okay, I'm back now and feeling better. I got some toast to soak up the alcohol, so I can still eat and write at the same time. I'm actually pretty quick at one-handed typing while I eat. Trade secret.

Sunday comes, right? A week after I'd met this guy. I was planning on going down to Cool Beans at 10:30 and luring him to some secluded place so I could give him a proper beating and find out who he really was.

I never got the chance to; instead, I woke up Sunday morning by an insistent knocking on my door.

"I'm coming, I'm coming," I yelled, getting out of bed to put my shirt on. Blood vessels in my head felt like they were going to explode. Turning around, I saw a red 8:08 on the digital clock. Who in their right mind would be knocking on a hotel room door this early on a Sunday morning?

I peeked through the peephole. "Oh, that's who," I whispered to myself.

Unlatching the deadbolt, I opened the door to the bright-eyed man, standing there in the same attire from last week. The grinning pig on the front of his shirt mimicked his own round, bearded smile.

"Jack! Good morning!" he said, walking right through the door without even asking for permission. He surveyed the hotel room, the bottles, and me standing there in my boxers, a v-neck white t-shirt, hair everywhere. "Partying it up by yourself, huh, Jack?"

I wore a dumb hungover stare on my face. "Kind of depressing, if you ask me," he said.

I reared back, took aim and swung what I thought was a mean right hook at him. The thing is, though, I missed. He didn't move a muscle. I just plain old missed. And I wound up in the floor beside the overturned table that I fell on and knocked over, an empty beer bottle on my chest.

He bent over laughing, gasping and slapping his knees. "Ah-ha-ha...whoa there, Mike Tyson! Easy!" He walked over and offered his hand to help me up, but I refused it. He just stood there. I was too dizzy to get up by myself. So I just lay there. In my v-neck and boxers, smelling like beer. Classy. He stared at me and smiled.

"Who are you and how did you know about my affair?" I mumbled through the grog.

"Well," he said, putting his hands on his hips. "I'm not sure if you're ready for this, but you are laying in the floor in your underwear decorated with beer bottles, so I guess now is as good a time as any." He smiled at that. "My name is Yeshua, like I told you. It's Hebrew. But you would know me as Jesus. I'm Jesus. You know, from the Bible. But you can still call me Yeshua if you want. I'll answer to either."

"Did you just say that you are Jesus, like, from the Bible?" I said.

"Yes."

"Shit." I said, putting my right hand over my face and rubbing my eyes. "I must be really hungover."

He thought that was funny, evidently, because he started belly laughing again. "Yes, yes, you are pretty hungover Jack. As evidenced by your, um, knockout punch there."

He laughed again.

I didn't.

"But you aren't crazy, you aren't drugged, and you aren't dreaming. I really am Jesus. I'm here to talk to you. About your column and your life. After all, you said I seemed like a pretty cool guy that you'd like to hang out with, right?"

"Yeah, I did, didn't I?" But I don't read guy meets God novels, and I certainly don't live them, I thought. "Did you ride your donkey over here from Nazareth or just take the stairway from heaven?"

"You're a funny guy, Jack." He was still smiling. "A bit snooty too, but regardless, we don't really have time for goofing around this morning. We've got places to be," he said.

"Okay, really, who are you? Who put you up to this? Who is punking me? You can tell them that I've already told my wife about the affair. So tell them thanks, they should be happy now—they got me kicked out of my house and now I live in this dump."

"Sure, right. Your inability to keep your pants on is what got you kicked out of your house, Jack. And rightly so." I didn't have anything to say really after that, and I realized that I was still lying in the floor. So I mustered up the strength to stand up, without his help of course, propping myself on the table. Still a bit woozy.

"I'm calling the cops," I said, reaching for my phone.

"I wouldn't do that."

"Why?"

"What are you gonna tell them? That you're drunk, you let a man into your hotel room, then tried to assault him—only to destroy hotel property because of your intoxication?"

I couldn't think of a response to that.

"Well, if you are really Jesus—" I said.

"Oh, no. We don't have time for that." He cut me off. "Hmm," he said to himself. "How can I spare you the whole 'If you're really God do something crazy to prove it' speech…" He looked as if he had found the answer.

He walked over to me, put his hand on my shoulder and I swear he almost teared up. "I'm really sorry about what your Uncle Richard did to you."

My breath left me. "What did you say?" My heart started knocking on my ribcage. I wanted to kill him. I wanted to choke the life out of his throat for even saying Uncle Richard's name. Whoever he was, he shouldn't have known that. If he wasn't Jesus, then who the hell was he to say anything about what happened? If he was Jesus, he should have stopped it from happening. But I couldn't move; I couldn't think of any words to say. I knew that the only people on earth that knew about Uncle Richard were my mother and Sara. My mother was dead and Sara would never do something like this.

Hence the freak out.

"Well, I don't think you should go out in public like that," he broke the silence and I saw my bed hair in the mirror, realizing how truly awful I looked for the first time. "So why don't you go take a hot shower and sober up real quick, and then we'll get going."

"Okay," was all I could muster. I looked back at him, grabbed my clothes and went to the bathroom to start the water. I rubbed my eyes really hard and pinched myself several times in the shower, trying to figure out if I was crazy or drugged or dreaming. I felt fine though, with the hangover receding by the minute. I dried off and put my pants on, then cracked the door open a tad.

"Are you still there?" I asked, steam pouring past my head and into the cool room.

"Yep, still here." He was sitting in the chair, feet propped up on the table, arms crossed.

"Are you still Jesus, from the Bible? I mean…Yeshua?"

"Yep," he said, laughing. "Last time I checked."

"I don't believe you," I said.

He winked at me, then went on. "I don't expect you to believe me yet. But you will one day."

I shut the door back and walked over to the mirror, wiping a circle to see my face in. I stared at my reflection, realizing that nothing in the past week seemed real—prayer groups on Facebook, getting kicked out of my own house, breaking up with Jordan—and all of it was because of this stupid homeless man pretending to be Jesus.

Suddenly, a tremendous POW! rang in my ears and the door behind me as though the building was falling.

I screamed like a little girl and fell to the floor.

Not exactly my finest moment.

When I finally realized that the world hadn't ended and opened the door, I saw the old man standing there, dying laughing.

"What the hell was that?"

He mimicked kicking the door with his foot. "Pow!" he said, and gave a little scream, mocking my terror. "Gotcha!"

21

So maybe you had this figured out already, this "Yeshua" being Jesus and all. Maybe you're ready to toss this letter aside and write me off as a crackpot. I would. And maybe you're thinking, there's no way you'd go along with this guy's charade, so why am I?

At this point, I didn't have much of a choice. I had no home, no family, nothing to do but play this one out. See what kind of freak this guy truly was.

As it turns out, a complete freak.

So we get in my car and start driving downtown—that's where he tells me to go. A few minutes later he directs me into a small parking lot of a building with a large glass front. Stenciled on the window in large white letters is a name with something about words of faith and prosperity in it. "We're going to church?" I ask.

"Something like that." We get out and walk to the front door—I notice there are only two other cars in the parking lot.

It doesn't take me long to figure out that we aren't in a church, but an office building. We walk past some gaudy pictures and fake palm trees before rounding the corner and entering a television studio.

And we are just in time for the show.

I look at Yeshua, incredulous. Are we here to listen to some televangelist hawk his snake oil? Am I supposed to "get saved" or something by his message? Thankfully I had left my checkbook back in the hotel room. The man looks exactly like your typical televangelist—down to the greasy hair, the golden cufflinks and the rapid rate of speech, like a swanky used car dealer. Maybe you've seen this guy on Sunday morning—I don't know what you normally do on Sunday mornings, but if you've ever turned on the TV while making breakfast or something, you've probably seen him.

So we were in the studio, and the guy stood behind his podium and preached like his paycheck depended on it, rattling off phrases like "claim your miracle today," and "you have to name God's promises and claim them over your life." It was no different than any other health and wealth late night television scam, except it seemed more desperate in person. For one, the studio was decorated in an almost painful way, with silly-looking tapestries and golden, regal looking columns that you could tell were made of styrofoam. And it looked like the cameraman doubled as the producer and only audience member.

After an inspiring moment in the message and a pause for effect, the cameraman leaned over to the soundboard and pressed a button for canned applause. That was about all I could take. I turned to Yeshua to try and figure out what we were doing in this pitiful place.

I'm not even turned around before I hear the guy at the podium ask "What are you doing?" like someone has just driven their car through his living room. Yeshua walks up to him, his back to the camera, and whispers something in his ear. The guy drops his hands to his sides, and Yeshua sits him down in his chair, pulls out two pairs of handcuffs and snaps down his forearms tight to the chair rail. I look around for the cameraman, but he's gone. And the "On Air" button is still lit.

Yeshua hands him a piece of paper. The man reads a bit silently, then starts to tear up a bit. Yeshua walks back over to him again, still not recognizable by the camera, and whispers to him again. The man blurts out, "Don't you know that the Bible says? 'Touch not the Lord's anointed?' I would be afraid if I were you mister. 'Vengeance is mine,' saith the Lord." His voice shook like a pubescent boy.

Yeshua grabs his left ear and twists it backwards in his palm while the man screams. Finally Yeshua says something: "Anointing with snake oil doesn't count." Then he lets go of his ear and steps away.

Can you imagine being some little old lady with her checkbook on her lap, ready to claim her miracle with a gift of $1000 or more, and seeing this on your tube Sunday morning?

After another moment, the man cleared his throat and started reading:

"I am a fake and a scoundrel, and I do not speak the truth of God. I selfishly prostitute the truth to benefit myself, and I use money from misled donors to fund my ridiculously lavish lifestyle." He looked so aghast; you would think he had seen Elvis.

He went on, "I have never once prayed over the vials of miracle water that I sell, and I trash every prayer request that I get in the mail. I am an unquenchably selfish and a pitiful liar, misleading well-meaning people and robbing them for years on end. I am sorry and I will pay back every penny that you have given me. I will write you a check immediately if you come up to my office right now."

He flipped at that last statement, his eyes as big and bright as oranges. Yeshua looked at him again and nodded for him to keep going.

He gave the address of the place and said, "I will be here all day, sitting right here in this spot."

He panicked and tried to get up from the chair, but he could only budge the chair, it was so heavy. Guess that splurge was a decision he regretted, huh?

"I am sorry for cheating you, and I know that the living God will deal with my sin accordingly. The heart that Christianity leads to is sacrificing what you have to help others in need, not giving money to a quack like me in the hopes that you will be blessed. I am sorry for misrepresenting God and his truth to you, and I will be here waiting if you want your money back." At this, he stopped reading and broke out crying—pretty dramatically, it seemed to me. I guess he was still live on TV and knew it.

Still in awe, I looked up and saw Yeshua walking up briskly to my other side, motioning me to turn and walk with him. "We better get out of here…this is probably going to get ugly." I agreed, followed him to the car and we hopped in.

Both of us laughed hysterically as we sped away. "That was awesome!" I said. We laughed and talked a bit more until I realized I didn't know where I was supposed to be going and asked him. He told me to go to Elmwood Cemetery. Whoever this guy was, he was entertaining to say the least.

22

I mean, you can't *buy* that kind of entertainment.

I didn't tell you about my first experience with a televangelist. It feels appropriate now.

I was maybe ten at the time. Mrs. Robinson, a family friend, was keeping Sara and me. She always offered because she said she loved the company anyway, and I think she meant it. We sat at the table doing homework and Sara said she was hungry. Mrs. Robinson opened the refrigerator and I had never seen it so scarce. Sara asked for ham or turkey but she said she was sorry, PB & J would have to do—that she hadn't had time to go to the grocery store.

I was old enough to know that that was a lie. All she had was time.

After finishing my sandwich, I shifted my chair a bit so I could see the TV from the table. There was a man with gelled black hair and a three-piece suit sitting behind a large desk. The room was peculiar, the furniture out of place and gaudy, much like the television studio Yeshua and I had just crashed. The ornate, golden chair that the man sat in rose above his head, and the man leaned over a large book on the desk and spoke passionately.

He said he knew a lot of people were hurting right now, physically and financially, but that he had a special message from *Gawd*. He started on this spiel about anointing and abundance and favor and that *Gawd* had a miracle in store for his listeners. Then he pulled out a green handkerchief and said that friend, it probably looked like an ordinary handkerchief.

I hated the way he kept calling me friend, and it did, in fact, look like an ordinary handkerchief. But he went on and explained that it was actually a special miracle green prosperity prayer cloth. That it was a touch point between him and *Gawd*, so it had some kind of magic voodoo powers or something. I rolled my eyes at him while he talked about the special anointing he had put on them. He said that *Gawd* wanted to use one of these to bring healing and prosperity into your life, and that he was going to step out on a limb of faith and send you one for absolutely free. Yep, free.

Then came the pitch. He wanted to send it for free, friend, but you do know about sowing and reaping, right? He would hate for you to miss your miracle and not give you a chance to sow into *Gawd's work*. So if you were serious about your breakthrough, you could sew a seed into his ministry. He gladly accepted credit cards, checks, and money orders.

When the show faded to a word from the local sponsor, I turned to see what Mrs. Robinson was doing, expecting her to be knitting like usual.

She was still seated in the recliner, her gaze glued to the TV, oblivious to me. Her eyes were glazed, and a tear trail ran down her cheek. Her hand reached up to wipe it away, gripping a familiar green handkerchief.

I guess *Gawd* didn't work, I thought to myself.

23

So, back to that Sunday.

We arrived at the cemetery to find a slew of cars and motorcycles lining the entryway. I thought someone important must have died. "Now we're going to a funeral?" I asked.

"We've got one more thing to attend to today." While he offered far less clarity than I'd hoped for, he didn't look like he was in the mood for talking, so I just kept following.

When we reached the top of the hill, I saw military attire everywhere in the sea of people still a ways off. I remembered the story in the paper this week about the two young brothers who had been killed in the Middle East.

There were so many people there that it took me a moment to notice the peculiarity of this particular gathering. First, I noticed the massive group of bikers, all lined up in a straight row, some on their bikes and some just standing there, leather clad. Almost all of them held large American flags up above them. Then, I gasped, realizing that they were a giant human shield, protecting the funeral goers from a group of protestors with picketing signs.

We drew closer and I lost my breath as I was able to read the signs. They proudly waved them in the air:

Fag Troops.

Thank God For IED's.

Hell Must Be Hot.

God Hates Fags.

God Hates The World.

God Hates America.

I had seen these people on TV before, some group from a small independent church out west. Yeshua did not say a word, and I realized we were walking straight toward them.

It was a rather small group, but nonetheless they were loud. And they had *kids* holding signs. Young kids.

My heart raced as we inched closer to them, because Yeshua was headed right for them and showed no signs of stopping. Potential headlines for this story began to whir through my mind. Then I thought how it would have been nice of Yeshua to explain what exactly our plan was here—was he going to join them? Or something else?

But within seconds he was toe to toe with the old man who was apparently their leader and staring him straight in the face, silent. It was an awkward few seconds and no one really seemed to know what to do. Including the man.

"What, boy, you got a problem, or are you coming to join us?" the old man spattered, then turned his head to spit on the ground. Yeshua said nothing, just stood still. His eyes were fierce and I was getting a little afraid. The bikers had gotten the protestors far enough away from the funeral that none of this was actually disturbing the funeral, but in our little corner of the cemetery, all eyes were on these two men.

The man still held his sign, which said, *God Hates You.* Then, with astounding quickness, Yeshua reached up, grabbed the sign out of the man's hand and swung it around, busting it over the man's head. The sign broke in two pieces and fell to either side of the man. He stood there nonetheless, still looking into Yeshua's eyes but obviously afraid to recoil, or even mutter a word for that matter.

"How dare you—" Yeshua started, gritting his teeth together in a pause. "How dare you bring your false teaching here and dance on the grief of a fellow human being. And to have the audacity to proclaim the exact opposite of what Scripture teaches? God takes no pleasure in the death of the wicked. You make out like you are some saint by distinguishing yourself from other 'sinners,' pretending that you are righteous. I know what you do in secret, and if you are not leaving by the time I count to five, I'm going to start naming stuff. Take your people and get out of here right now. Go home and actually read your Bible. And *repent*. One…two…"

The man frantically gathered his group and hurried them by leading the way out. "Three…four…drop your signs!" Yeshua yelled.

They all threw them down, half-jogging, half-stumbling away back to their cars, and Yeshua walked around, picking the signs up one by one and breaking them in half over his knee. Then he walked over and stuffed them in a trashcan beside a bench and sat down on it.

Eventually, I went and sat down beside him. He still looked upset and I didn't know what to say. A few of the bikers walked over to thank him and shake his hand.

We sat there and watched the funeral from afar in silence for a few moments after the bikers left. Although I took great joy in what had happened, the fact that it had to happen was still so disgusting that there was really nothing funny to be had in it.

Finally, he broke the silence. "It is almost crazy how many different ways humanity has distorted God's truth into destructive myths and misrepresented me. It breaks my heart and makes me angry at the same time."

"I can't even imagine that someone could do what these people are doing," I said.

"Unfortunately, there has been no lack of harm and confusion produced by people who claim to represent me but really don't. That's the reason a lot of people, especially in this country, look at what they see as Christianity and don't want anything to do with me because of it. That could be said of you, right Jack?"

"Sure, that's why I wrote that column. The church sucks at acting like the Jesus of the Bible. That is, 'you.'"

"The true church is definitely not perfect, but I love her dearly. She is growing and being purified by me around the world, and there are many places where she is such a beautiful force that it would move you to tears. The problem is, although some of her stains come from true believers, much of the bad rap that Christianity has gotten in America has actually come from impostors, people that claim to be a part of my church but in reality are far from understanding the gospel, much less living it. People like those protestors."

"What is it that Jon Stewart said about them? That they are no more a church than Church's Fried Chicken is a church?"

He grinned and said, "Oh, Jon Stewart. That guy kills me."

I smirked and winked at him, wanting to press him a bit on his act. "So Jesus likes Jon Stewart, huh? Interesting."

"What's not to like about Jon Stewart?" he responded, smiling back. "He's hilarious."

"Okay," I said. "Test: if you are Jesus then you'll know who I think is funnier, Jon Stewart or Stephen Colbert?"

He projected his voice into an impression of mine and said: "In quite a close race I would say Colbert edges out Stewart just a tad—but it may only be my own personal bias since he's from South Carolina."

"Cheater!" I said, getting up and waving my hand at him in the air. I had written that in a column over a year ago. "And hey," I said, turning back to him. "That whole shenanigan today was kind of violent. I expected Jesus to be a little more peaceful than that."

He smiled, knowing I was trying to catch him. "That's because you Americans think that Jesus is nothing but a lamb-holding hippie that wears sandals and a white robe and always looks like he just got out of the shower. But you don't read parts of the Bible like Revelation 19 where I'm a warrior king, riding a white horse with a sword coming out of my mouth and a tattoo on my thigh."

"That's kind of creepy that you have a tattoo on your thigh," I said, grinning and looking at his blue jean-covered leg. "What does it say?" He laughed and smacked my pointing finger away.

24

We stayed for a while longer while the funeral crowd slowly died down and people drove away. As I watched the family members get into the black limo, I said "I can't imagine the pain that those people must have felt looking up here at those hate-filled signs, claiming to be messages from God."

"I know. The thing I want you to learn from today, Jack, is that sin hurts."

"Sin hurts," I repeated. "I thought only dancing, drinking, smoking, and sex hurt people."

He rolled his eyes at me.

"Many people think that sin is just the fun, bad stuff that people really want to do but they aren't supposed to for some reason, because God is a cosmic killjoy or something. But the opposite is actually true. God created humanity to experience joy through a perfect relationship with himself and with each other. You can't imagine how good that would be, to live in a world with no death or sickness, no lies, no abandonment, no rapes, murders or burglaries—no reason whatsoever to not fully trust every person you meet. But instead of living in that glorious world, you all chose to rebel against me and go your own way, to try to be equal with me in your pride instead of living in the humble glory I created for you. You traded dependence for independence, and perfect joy for a life of fruitless pursuits, chasing after mirages. And all of this has done nothing but cause an inexpressible amount of hurt in the world."

"I can see that." I paused. "That makes a nice little Sunday School lesson too, doesn't it? Are we gonna make our craft now or go to snack time?"

He glared at me, and I saw a glimpse of the angry heat he had for the protestors back there. For a second I almost thought he was going to name what I do in secret, but thankfully he rolled his eyes at me. "All right, smarty-pants—let's try another route. Let's make this personal. Do you remember when you and Chloe were first married?"

"Of course."

"Was marriage good then? Did you enjoy it?"

"Yes."

"So did you ever love Chloe?"

"Of course I loved Chloe. I still do."

"Do you have any idea how much she is hurting right now?" I sat in silence. "Do you? She trusted you with her life. Till death do you part. She gave you her heart, and you played with it. You did that to your *wife*—"

"Shut up!" I screamed at him, becoming red all over.

"I've got a Sunday School lesson to give you, remember?" He paused again. "I'm gonna tell you why you did this. Are you ready? Because you are insatiably selfish. You care about what you want more than anything in the world. Even if it almost kills the woman you promised your life to." He was really starting to piss me off. "Sin is essentially narcissism," he went on, "and recent events show that you only have eyes for your own reflection.

"So let's backtrack," he continued. "First we have the televangelist. What is his angle? 'Screw everyone but me—my gain is what is important and I'll twist anything I have to get it.'"

Pause.

"Now, let's talk about Jack Bennett. Getting what you want, not caring who it hurts. 'I know I'm married, but I want to sleep with other women, and I do what I want,'" he said, imitating me. "And the reason you are so angry at me is because you know it's true. And it's not just you Jack," he continued softly. "It's everyone —the entire human race, everyone has been in this revolt of self-interest. Everyone has given the finger to God, and anyone else in the way of the pursuit to get what they want—the thing they think is better than God and his idea for the world. This epidemic of selfishness is why the world is so deeply broken. Neglectful parents. Sexual abuse. Rape. Burglaries. Affairs. Extortion. Drunk drivers. All doing exactly what they want to do with no concern for others. I know you see this, Jack—"

I didn't respond. I don't think I physically could have said anything even if I'd wanted to.

"Your marriage to Chloe is a picture—a shadow of the perfect relationship I designed to have with humanity. And your betrayal of her is a picture of the sin of every human being against God. Not some impersonal *breaking of the rules*—it is a *relational betrayal*. A knife in the back of God and the perfect existence of his design and presence, just like your affair was a knife in the back of Chloe and the life that she wanted with you.

"You have certainly received your fair share of scars from other people's sin, Jack. And for that I am truly sorry. I hate the effects of sin as much as you do, I promise. But you have to own up to the fact that you've given out some scars too." I wrenched at his statement, and my heart sunk as I thought about what I had done to Chloe, to our family. I pictured her sitting on the bed right now, tissues wiping wet eyes. I thought back to meeting her at Denny's in college, to our wedding day, to the day we found out about the boys. Things were so good for so long. I'm not sure exactly what happened, but I know it was all my fault. The sense of something missing. The wandering eyes and desire for whatever emotional high that comes along with the unknown or mysterious. The incessant justifications. Reality rushed over me, and I began to realize just how selfish and stupid I had been.

I thought about Chloe's laugh and the boys running around in the yard, and I started, for the first time, to really understand what I had done and hate it.

I mean, really *hate* it.

"I am such an idiot," I said, putting my head down and breaking the silence.

"I won't argue with you there. Can I show you where you were headed?"

"I guess," I said, not really knowing what he meant. Was this going to be some sort of *It's A Wonderful Life*-style vision from Jesus?

"Close your eyes," he said. "Hit the fast forward button fifteen years and picture your family sitting at the dinner table. Chloe is there, elegantly aged but beautiful as ever, dipping a serving spoon in the mashed potatoes. Liam and Isaac are there, strong, handsome young men—football players just like you. Now notice the empty chair where you are not sitting, and think about the hole that you have from growing up without a father, and think about that same burden being on them—"

"No!" I interrupted, standing up and pointing my finger in his face. "How dare you? I would never, ever leave my children like my father left me. Never! I would still live in their city, still see them on weekends, still be at football games, still be there on their wedding day. How dare you insinuate that I would abandon them?"

He sat in silence for a moment and let me cool down as I paced. Finally, he spoke. "Blinded, Jack. Blinded. You were blinded by your selfishness, and Jordan was quickly becoming the thing you would chase, worship, and sacrifice anything for. Anything. You were quickly heading down the same exact road that your father took so many years ago, bound to end up a disappointed, bitter man whose idol did not deliver on its promises."

I wanted to keep screaming at him, but he was right. Something deep inside me told me it was true, because of the certainty I'd had that I'd finally found the thing that was missing in my life in Jordan. I sat motionless in the grass of that lonely cemetery, staring into space like a zombie. I had become my dad and fleshed out my own worst nightmare.

After a moment, Yeshua came and put his hand on my back. "It happens more than you think, Jack. You are a relational people. Because of the family structure, too often sins get passed along from generation to generation. Alcoholics raise kids who turn to alcohol. Abused kids turn into abusers. Identity issues and a million other things get passed down the line. But it doesn't have to be that way. The chain can be broken. I can heal the most broken people and free the heaviest chains. The picture you saw is where you were going, but it is not where you must go."

He raised his hand off my back. A minute or so later I sat up, turned around and realized he was gone. After a bit, I got up and walked about two hundred yards to the other side of the cemetery. I sat down in my usual spot beside her tombstone, and talked to her just like I had done so many times before. "I've been such a moron," I said, gritting my teeth and trying to hold back moisture from my eyes. "What a mess I've gotten myself into."

25

I should probably tell you what happened to my mom.

It was a little over three years ago, and Chloe and I were just about to sit down and watch a movie when my cell phone rang. It was Jenna, one of Sara's best friends.

I answered quickly, "Hey Jenna, everything okay?"

"Jack...it's Sara. She's not doing well. She called me a while ago really upset, saying she'd taken a bunch of sleeping pills. I rushed over to her apartment and made her throw them up, but she is still hysterical. She drove down to Group Therapy to get a drink, and I followed her here. I know she has drugs in her car, and I think you need to come quick."

I called Mom on the way to the bar to tell her what was going on. Sara would always resist her, but somehow Mom was always the one that would break through to her when things went bad. She said she would drive down as fast as she could and hung up the phone.

Chloe and I pulled up to Group Therapy and ran in. Sara was sitting in a dark corner booth near the bar, eyes wet with tears, Jenna right beside her. She had a gin and tonic in her hand, and she looked up at me as Chloe and I sat down. She was skeleton thin and her veins showed more than they should. She had always been gorgeous, but more and more it had grown into that sad kind of beauty. "Sara, babe—are you okay? Did something happen?"

She said nothing, only fidgeted her drink with her bony fingers. Jenna stroked her hair, and after a moment spoke, "She just told me that she caught Ben cheating on her with another girl." At that, Sara's mouth tightened and she turned her head away.

"Again? Sara," I said, gently as possible. "How many times do I have to tell you? Forget about him—you deserve so much better. Why do you keep going back to him?"

"I love him," she answered, quivering. "I don't know why I do, but I do."

"Well, he doesn't love you," I answered harshly. "Because if he did he would straighten up, get a job that would provide for you, treat you like you deserve to be treated and make a good life for you."

"A good life," she said, smirking at the idea with her tone and her dark smile. "You think that a good life is out there for me, Jack? I'm not sure there is such a thing anymore. And there aren't many good guys out there. They just want to use you and abuse you, but still keep you around in case they need you."

"Sara, there are plenty of great guys out there who would love you well and treat you like the princess you are," Chloe chimed in, pleading with her. "Please don't go back to him. Come home with us tonight, please. We'll go get something to eat and go home and watch a movie—we'd love to have you stay with us for as long as you want. You can get away from these people who are bringing you down and start again." Chloe looked at me and I shrugged. Who knew if she was getting through to her? "I'd love to have some help painting the nursery for the boys, you know. We've got a lot of work to do to get ready for them and they sure are going to love their Aunt Sara."

Brilliant, I thought. Chloe always knew exactly what to say. I saw the faintest smile flash across Sara's face as she looked at Chloe's stomach. But the smile quickly turned downward, and then to a flood of tears. All of us reached out to touch her, begging her to tell us what was wrong. Finally, she managed to get out some mumbled words. "We were pregnant—last Christmas Eve, I…he wanted me to abort it." She sobbed through the sentences and we held her around that awkward bar table until she couldn't cry anymore. My heart was broken for her more than it ever had been, and it was all I could do to hold back tears. She tried to dry up and I held my hand on her back, telling her that it was okay and that we loved her no matter what. The despair in her eyes was unlike anything I'd ever seen.

"Please tell me you didn't call Mom," Sara asked. "I really don't feel like getting religion tonight." In the past few years, Mom had joined a small church near her house. She didn't push anything on us too hard, though.

We were interrupted by a familiar buzzing, and as I got my phone out of my pocket I realized I had several missed calls. The number was unknown.

"Yes, Sara she is coming. You know it wouldn't be a real party unless she was here…" Everyone giggled a little bit at that and the mood lightened. My phone rang again and I was too curious not to answer.

"Hello?"

"Is this Jack Bennett?"

"Yes…may I ask who is calling?"

"This is the Columbia Police Department. Are you April Bennett's son?"

"Yes I am—is something wrong?"

"She has been involved in a car accident. Can you please come up to the intersection of Assembly and Whaley?"

She had been t-boned by some stupid drunk college student at the intersection. I got there, jumped out of my car and, pushing back the EMT, ran straight to her stretcher. The lights swirling and the firemen cleaning up the debris all looked like they were in slow motion. I finally got to the stretcher and pulled back the white sheet and lifted her bloody head to my chest. I held her and ran my fingers through her hair and begged her to wake up until I finally gave up. A few cops eventually pulled me away from her body. I am thankful that evidently my emotions were so strong I cannot remember it clearly. It's a good thing, because I wouldn't want my lasting memory of her to be that bloody mess, but the lighthearted laugh and shining smile I remember from telling her jokes as a little boy.

I miss her so much, that irreplaceable saint.

Death is such a bitch, isn't it? It's wrong. All wrong. There is something about the essence of life that seems inevitably eternal, like a flame that cannot be put out. Don't tell me you don't understand that—all you have to do is look into someone's eyes. I've heard people say that the eyes are the window to the soul. I think that is stupid and cheesy and incredibly true. That is where I see the spark, and you know what I'm talking about. I've seen that spark in your eyes. That's why I'm telling you all of this. Because there's a part of you that is more than just living and dying.

And well, the reality of seeing someone, the invincible fire of life dancing in their eyes, and then the next time you see them they are dead—eyes cold, brown, motionless? It's just too much to handle. Wrong in the worst sense of the word.

And then you have their things, the things that could not be anyone's but theirs and will always remind you of them and that they should still be alive to own. And you have their clothes. Their clothes with their smell on them. And you can pick up the shirt that was on top of the clothes hamper and hold it up to your nose and you feel them in and all around you, except they aren't there. They are still the pale shell that just got driven away to the funeral home.

It's too much.

I'm sure you know what I mean. I'm sure you have lost dearly loved people. I am sorry.

Death makes you feel your mortality like nothing else can. I mean, right now I sit here writing this letter to you—my hands work fine and are full of typing fury, my mind sparks and calls things to mind, etc. But thinking about the fact—unalterable—that one day this body of mine, which feels very much my own and very much like it could go on living forever and really doesn't even get the fact that it won't somehow—will be a lifeless shell? That is disturbing. I can't really fathom my body keeling over and not being alive anymore. What does that mean for me?

The other thing death does to you is that it makes you realize how very little control you actually have. Think about it—we have doctors, hospitals, medicine, safe cars with airbags and seat belts, and all the things that should make us as safe as possible and prolong our lives. We trust in these things, but in the end they are always reduced to fool's gold—all have the end of their ropes. None of them have ever kept anyone alive forever. To realize that, all you have to do is have a doctor tell you, "Sorry, we have done everything we can," or see that seat belt that makes you feel so safe holding up someone's limp body.

I miss my Mom. I want to hug her right now, wrap my arms around her frail little body and smell her VO hairspray and tell her how much I love her and how thankful I am for her. I want to tell her thanks for working so hard for all those years to support us, because I never did tell her that. I want to hear her laugh and watch her run around with my boys—my beautiful boys that she never got a chance to hold. They would love her so much.

26

Before I found you today, I'd occasionally have dreams about you, but I still never saw anything but your eyes. I'd try to use my imagination and draw in your face but it never worked. And the tears, so many tears, the ugly weight of desperation that we shared.

I felt so sorry for you.

Dreams can really suck sometimes.

Sometimes when I get sad, I YouTube videos of babies laughing. It may be superficial, and you may think I'm strange (and I won't argue with you), but it helps. There's this one with this baby sitting in a high chair, food caked on her face, and she's so excited about the idea of taking a bath. She says, "Bath? Bath? Bath? Bath?" over and over again, and then laughs at the end.

It's the best thing ever.

Or, I'll watch that incredible a cappella version of the song "Africa" by Toto where they start out making that thunderstorm. Have you ever seen that? It's pretty incredible. And then there's the kid's choir from New York that sings the song about New York by Jay-Z and Alicia Keys. YouTube can really be a pal to lift your spirits when you need it.

Okay, enough of that for now. Let's recap.

I write a column about how Christianity is messed up. A week later I meet a homeless guy who's locked out of a church, and he tells me to end my affair. Then the next week he comes to my hotel room and tells me that he's Jesus while I'm lying on the floor with a killer hangover. He's full of shit, but I want to humor him and see where it leads. We start doing all this crazy stuff and I kind of start to like him. Pile all of this on top of the fact that I had just alienated the two closest people in my life and I couldn't see my boys. You can probably imagine my mental state at this point.

So I went to see Sara that week. It was the first time I had done that in quite a while, to be honest.

I walked up to her apartment and knocked on the door. "Hey there, baby sister."

"Oh. Hey Jack. I haven't seen you in months. Come on in." She gave me an awkward side hug and I went and sat on the couch.

"You want some coffee?"

"Sure, I'd love some."

"Black, right?"

"Yeah," I said.

I think it's important for you to know that I drink my coffee black. I have been quite proud of that for about a year now. It only took me two weeks to get over that disgusting cream and sugar crap.

Sara poured both of us a cup of coffee and strolled over to sit down across from me on a recliner. "So, what's new with you, sis? Are you still working at American Apparel?"

"Yep, sure am," she said, sipping her coffee.

"You're managing now, right? Making pretty good money it seems." I looked around the apartment.

"Yeah I am—the money's not bad. Not great for as much as I work though."

"I know the feeling." I spun my coffee mug around in my hand. "So, are you doing okay? You're not, um...are you?"

"No Jack, I'm not. Thanks for asking, though," she said quickly, a little cold.

"I really like what you've done with the place. Very modern. Sleek. I love it."

"Thanks. I try," she said, attempting a smile.

"Are you still seeing that guy? What's his name?"

"Aaron. Yes, I'm still seeing him."

"That's good," I answered, a bit awkwardly.

I didn't even remember the guy's name that my sister had been dating for close to a year. "Is he treating you well?"

"Sure," she said, without any clarification.

"Any wedding bells in the near future?"

"I doubt that," she answered. "Not anytime soon at least. Not sure he's ready for that. Or me either, for that matter."

"Yeah, no reason to rush."

"What about you Jack? What brings you by here? There has to be something on your mind for a surprise visit?"

"I can't just drop by and see my little sister?"

"You can. But you don't. So what's up?"

How do you respond to that? I took a deep breath and prepared myself. "I just wanted to stop by and talk. Well, you see…" I was nervous. "I've been having an affair with a girl from work."

"Shut up!" she said, anger and disappointment oozing from her voice. "After how good Chloe has been to you? And the boys?" She cursed me and asked me what I was thinking.

"I know, I know," I said, trying to calm her down. "I know I have been an absolute moron."

"Please tell me Chloe knows already. Please."

"Yes, yes, she knows. I told her last week. And I broke it off with the other girl."

She stared at me. "What the hell, Jack?"

"I know. It's the biggest regret of my life."

"How is Chloe handling it? Are you still staying at home?"

"What do you think?"

She just shook her head in disgust.

"And no, I'm not staying at home. I'm over at the Extended Stay Motel for now."

Sara looked down at the floor, face in her hands. "If you weren't my big brother, I'd punch you in the face."

"I know, Sara. I deserve it. I'm doing everything I can to make it right."

"You better be," she said, looking up at me. "Or I'll kill you." She was only halfway joking. She thought for a moment, then spoke, "Jack, there's no reason for you to pay money to stay at a hotel. Go grab your stuff and come back here. You can stay with me until you get things worked out."

"No, Sara, that's not why I came—I'm not going to do that."

"No, really," she said. "I want you to. Here. Here is a key." She pulled a key off of her key ring and put it on the glass coffee table. "In fact, you have to—so I can keep you straight. Your curfew is 9:00 every night."

I took a deep breath but didn't say anything.

"The spare bedroom is back there," she pointed down the hall. "I've got to go to work, so I'll see you soon." She got up and took our coffee mugs over to the sink. "You better be here tonight when I get home. Or else." She half-smiled and with that, walked back to her bedroom to get ready for work.

Oh, I forgot to tell you one thing. On the way to Sara's apartment that day, I was sitting at a red light on Assembly and I just happened to look over to my right and notice a guy on a motorcycle. I've never been much of a motorcycle guy, but I kind of wish I was. I think I'd look pretty good on a motorcycle. So I'm looking at this guy, noticing the man's blue jeans and shirt, and I suddenly glimpse his face and realized that it's the guy. Jesus. The light turns green and he takes off, so I decide to stay a ways behind him and follow so I could see where he is going and try to figure out what his game is.

I wasn't as smooth as I thought, because I soon realized he was going in circles. He finally stopped beside me at another red light, looked over at me, and smiled like he knew exactly what I was doing. I kept following for another few blocks just to mess with him, but then I gave up.

But—what's a homeless guy pretending to be Jesus riding around on a motorcycle for?

27

I don't know why I am telling you this part. There's no need to really. This whole honesty thing is going a little far, but for some reason it is just coming out of me.

Talk about being an absolute moron.

That same day—the day I went to Sara's—yeah, I did something stupid. Something else stupid would be a more accurate description. I never told Sara. She really would have killed me I think.

Literally on my way back to the hotel from Sara's to grab my stuff and check out, Jordan calls me. And I pick up. First mistake. We have some awkward small talk and then she says she has a small favor to ask—she needs help moving a new TV stand and has no one around. I hesitated but finally agreed to stop by real quick. I think you can figure out the rest from there. No need for details.

Even after getting called out by a complete stranger on my affair, after confessing to Chloe and to Sara, after the talk on Sunday and the thoughts of me turning into my dad. The depths of my stupidity never cease to amaze me. Honestly.

After going to Jordan's and then grabbing my stuff from the hotel, I was on my way to Sara's apartment. While driving I had probably the most clear breakthrough moment, where everything just kind of hit me and I had to pull over because I was so overwhelmed. I don't know how to describe it really. It's like I just woke up. Like I was asleep somehow before, and the light bulbs just came on. It started with the question: "What are you doing with your life, Jack?"

You know what I think one of the toughest parts of life to deal with is? Expectations. Or unmet expectations, rather, which most expectations turn out to be in my experience. I realized this, maybe more so than I ever have, at a wedding I was in a while back. It was a college buddy who was getting hitched, and I was a groomsman. The ceremony was fairly short and sweet—your typical southern wedding—but during the service I could not keep my eyes off of this one bridesmaid. I know what you are thinking, and I'm not talking about that kind of staring. She was pretty, but no, not what I mean. I mean that I could not turn away from the way this wedding was affecting her.

I didn't know her—she was in her thirties and I had met her family at the rehearsal the night before. Husband, young son and younger daughter. A beautiful, all-American family. The daughter happened to be the flower girl as well, so the whole service the lady stood there, the maid of honor I guess you call it, with her daughter standing in front of her in a pristine, frilly white dress. And though I usually focus on the couple getting married during weddings, I couldn't help but notice this woman.

Anyway, for some reason I felt like I was experiencing the wedding through her eyes. The plastic, made up smile that was painted on her face said one thing, but her eyes—they said something very different. I saw her going back, picturing her own wedding day and reliving the excitement and the pomp. And then I saw her fast-forwarding through the subsequent years of marriage and her life now. And her eyes seemed to say that it was all a lie. That the dreams, the hopes and expectations—the "happily-ever-after"—that it was all a lie and that the brevity of its scope would make you want to weep at the next wedding you attended.

It made me terribly sad for her.

If you are doubting whether I could discern all of this from the look in her eyes, I understand. I could be wrong. But I'm usually not about these things. Reading people has always been my gift, I guess.

Be warned, I can read you like a book. You won't be able to keep any secrets from me.

I understand where she is coming from. I feel like I have gone throughout life, from one thing or stage to the next, always with this weight of expectation of how things are going to be when I get to the next phase and how good it is going to be. And it is nearly always a significant disappointment. The excitement wears off, the new and shiny fades. I don't know what this means. I do know that disappointment seems to be a common thread of human experience though, does it not?

Is this true for you too? Did you ever think you would turn out to be as scarred as you are? As bitter or unstable? It seems an unfortunate reality of life that you will likely end up doing things you never thought you'd do, if you are like me, at least. You will say things you never thought you'd say, and things will be true of your life that you never wanted or thought possible.

Oh, the existential suck of life.

In a related way, this is what happened to me that day in my car. Pulled over on the side of the road, I began to run through in my mind all the expectations and dreams of my life that I had developed over the years. And then I juxtaposed them with the reality of what I had turned out to be, and I almost had a panic attack. Maybe. I'm not really sure what that would be like, but it freaked me out in a bad sort of way.

What had I done with my life? I certainly had not turned out the way I had hoped. Having a secret affair for months. Lying so often and well that it scared me. Neglecting my kids. Even confessing to my wife, only to run back and screw around at the drop of a hat.

Not to mention the failed dreams. I had wanted to be a writer. Turns out I can't write a plot to save my life, but I can write opinion pieces for a newspaper. Woo-hoo, look at me go! I tried to write a novel once, and my main character kept running off to Acapulco to drink tequila on the beach. Which was fun and all, but not a very interesting story.

I wanted to do something meaningful with my life—to be remarkable at something. At anything, really. To be Jack Bennett, that guy that's an outstanding _____. I had accomplished being an average columnist at best, a pitiful father, and well, you know what kind of husband I'd been. And I didn't have a clue what I thought was meaningful anymore.

28

So I decided I had to talk to Chloe. I'd called her several times since I'd been kicked out, but guess what, she didn't answer. Couldn't blame her. I left a note for Sara on the counter, telling her what I was doing, and I arrived at my house around eight. For a while I sat there fidgeting with my key ring trying to build up courage. I took a deep breath, got out, and walked slowly toward the front door. My memories chased me and barraged my brain the entire way.

The day we found this house.

The day we moved in.

The night we found out we were pregnant. We jumped around for an hour like teenage girls.

When we found out we were having twins and freaked out for a week.

Our sixth anniversary dinner on the front porch because we couldn't find a baby-sitter.

The countless times the boys had chased and tackled me in the front yard.

When I got to the front door I knocked gently. I knew the boys would be in the bed by now and hoped to talk to Chloe.

Thirty seconds passed, then a minute, then three minutes. I knocked again, a little harder. A little time passed, and then I heard footsteps coming toward the door. Chloe lifted up one blind to peer out, saw it was me, and then the porch light went dark and she walked away.

I knocked again. "Chloe, please open the door. Please. I just want to talk. I'm not leaving here until I get to see you. I'll sit out here all night if I have to. Please just let me talk to you."

I knew she heard me, so I turned around and sat down in the rocking chair beside the door on the porch. I began to rock back and forth, and the memory train began once again. If I knew Chloe, I would be out here for a while. I shivered and zipped up my fleece, glad I'd decided to bring it.

I sat for a while in my thoughts before I was startled by the brightness of the porch light. The door unlocked behind me, but it remained closed. I looked down at my watch and saw that it was 10:03. I sighed because, well, thirty minutes in the cold would have said, "You're in trouble buddy," an hour would have said "I'm still really, really pissed," and two hours…well, you know what two hours says.

I got up, gently opened the door, and smelled my house for the first time in over a week. I closed it gently behind me and saw Chloe sitting on the couch in our living room, knees pulled up and her arms around them. I walked into the living room as if I were being careful not to step on a landmine, and stood there in a dumb silence.

"Are you gonna just stand there like an idiot or are you gonna say something?" Oh Chloe, how I had missed her bluntness. "And sit down, you are making me nervous." I sat down on the love seat adjacent from her, leaning forward with my hands resting on my knees.

"Chloe," I had this speech all planned out, but my mind was trying to play tricks and confuse me. "Um, I know there are really no words I can say that mean much right now. But I just want you to know how sorry I am. I am utterly disgusted with myself—"

"Well that makes two of us," she interrupted with a bite.

"I know Chloe. I promise I am more upset and sorry about this than you probably think. I have been an absolute moron and I really don't know what I was thinking. I've been blinded by stupidity and selfishness and it makes me sick to think about how much I have hurt you."

"So are you still with that skank? I knew she was a whore the first time I met her."

"No, honey—"

"Don't call me honey. I'm not your honey anymore."

"I am not with her anymore. I completely broke it off like I told you. This wasn't her fault, it was mine. I don't want her. I want you. And I will do anything to get you back."

"And how am I supposed to believe that, Jack? Obviously that ring on your finger didn't mean anything three weeks ago, how do I know it will mean something in the future?"

"I'm different now. I'm seeing things more clearly and I really do know how stupid I've been. I don't want to be that person anymore. I've realized how much I really love you and our family, and how I don't want anything else through this. If you'll give me a chance I hope I can show you that."

She had emotions boiling all over her face, and for a moment I couldn't tell which one was going to steam. "I want to know when this all started. I want to know everything." Anger. It was anger.

I took a deep breath to prepare. This was going to lead nowhere good but I owed it to her. "The work trip to Charleston back in March. That's when we...well...for the first time."

Her eyes brewed angry tears. "So our anniversary on the front porch, one of my favorite memories ever—and you were sleeping with another woman!" She got up and started pacing around, fury in her light footsteps. I buried my head in my hands, muttering quietly, "I know. I am so sorry."

"And the last time, when was the last time you...were with her?" she said, standing still in the middle of the living room now, back turned to me.

Oh no. No. Not that question. I squirmed, "About a week ago, I guess."

Her eyes pounced on me like I was an injured antelope in the jungle. "You are a pitiful liar, Jack. Tell me the truth."

Oh my. "About two hours ago." She snarled and started to cry again, but then halfway laughed in this furious outburst that I don't know how to describe. Hysterical is a good word I guess. Yeah, let's go with hysterical.

"You are such a worthless piece of shit, Jack. What was I thinking when I married you?"

"I am so, so sorry. I promise I am finished—done. Never again. I know that words can't describe what I have done. That's why I came now, because things really are different and that is a promise."

"Your promises don't mean much." She was getting every ounce of burn in her voice possible. "You know what I was doing two hours ago? Never mind. What do you care?"

And you might not believe me; I don't know how I knew it. I just did. "You were taking a pregnancy test." I looked up at her.

She took a step back, stunned. "How did you know? Did Mom call you?"

"No. I just now realized it. I should have known—I missed the signs somehow."

"Maybe because you were too busy screwing another woman? That could've had something to do with it."

"Yeah." What else could I say?

"Mommy?" We both looked over to the hallway to find Liam standing in the doorway. His blonde curls were disheveled and he held Peter the panda by his left side. My mom had saved it all those years.

My heart raced seeing him for the first time in way too long.

Chloe dried up as much as possible and went over to pick him up. He was clearly worried about her.

"Mommy's okay, sweetheart, don't you worry," she said as she hoisted him to her side. His eyes were still adjusting to the light when he noticed me and let out a sleepy yell, "Daddy!" He got down and ran over to my arms and I hugged my little boy. "Where you been Daddy?"

"I've been away working buddy. I sure have missed you though." I said, trying to keep my eyes dry. "Have you and your brother been good for Mommy?"

"Yeah."

"Good," I said, pushing back his hair and kissing him on the forehead.

"Come Liam, it's time for you to get back in the bed." Chloe said, motioning for him. He started towards her, then stopped and faced me. "Daddy, see you morning?"

"Uh…" I stammered, "I don't know, buddy. Maybe I can at least take you and Isaac to the park tomorrow night?" I looked up at Chloe, hoping she wouldn't be angry at the suggestion.

Liam jumped up and down, "Yeah, yeah. The park!" Chloe gave me a look but didn't object, so I told him I would see him tomorrow night and kissed him goodnight, glad he was too little to understand what was going on. Chloe grabbed him by the hand and led him back towards their bedroom. I wanted to punch myself while watching them walk away.

She came back a few moments later and sat back down on the couch in silence. She wasn't as upset after the interruption, but I didn't want to risk setting her off again, so I didn't say anything. I was content to sit in the hope of silence for the moment.

"Not exactly the way I pictured my life playing out," she finally said, curling the left corner of her mouth.

"Yeah. I know. I am so sorry. I wish like anything that I could take it back, but I know that's not possible. The only thing I can ask for is for you to give me another chance if you can. I promise to love you better and be a better husband to you than I've ever been. And I know it won't be an automatic thing where we can just go back to the way things used to be. I know you'll need some time, and I'll give you all the time you need. I'm not going anywhere, and I really mean it that I've realized the only thing I want is you."

She sat quietly for a moment. "So what is it about me that wasn't good enough for you, Jack?"

"Nothing, no, that's not it at all." Her words made me hurt for her even worse.

"No?" She looked at me, and I realized what this meant to her. This wasn't about me and my own crisis. All she could see was her own inadequacies and assume that she led me to this.

"No—no honey, absolutely not. There is nothing wrong with you. I love everything about you." I said shakily, feeling with each hollow but sincere line that I was losing her. She sat there, arms folded across her stomach and despair painting her face. Her years and years of self-image issues, the eating disorder that she battled through high school and college that almost took her life— she had come so far the past several years, and because of what I had done, those demons were back with a vengeance.

I got up quickly and walked over to the couch, getting on my knees in front of where she was sitting. "Chloe, please, no. It had nothing to do with you—you have always been and still are the woman of my dreams. It was all in me. Some sort of notion that I was missing something. I thought fulfilling my ambitions would help—promotions at work, having children, buying our house, buying nice stuff, but through all of that it only got worse. Then I convinced myself that maybe it was another person that would ful-fill it, but it was all a lie. I felt more empty and desperate with her than I ever have, but for some reason I just kept chasing it, kept believing the lies. I was blinded by my own self-absorption and it only made me more miserable. I am so, so sorry. Please don't be-lieve that this is somehow your fault. It was all my fault and you are way more than I deserve."

She looked at me through her tears and I knew that she heard me, but she didn't believe me. Not yet, at least. Those famili-ar, shaky eyes terrified me, testifying to the battle raging in her mind.

After a moment, she said, "I think you should go now." Most of the anger was gone from her voice by now, and all that was left was despair. I crawled up off my knees and stood up, try-ing to think of something to say. "Sure." I stood for a moment, then started walking awkwardly toward the door. "Oh," I said and stopped. "I know this won't mean much now, but I'm really excited about the baby."

She looked at me without smiling, then rolled her eyes and looked down, saying nothing. I turned the knob and opened the door. "Are you coming to get the boys tomorrow night?"

"Yes. I'll be here at six to pick them up. Thanks for letting me do that."

She nodded her head and I stepped out into the cold. I walked through my yard and got in my car, wishing for all the world that I was not leaving my house.

As I closed the door, someone rapped on my passenger window, and I jumped so high I almost hit my head on the roof.

29

Guess who it was. Right? It figures.

I rolled down my window to see Yeshua's face and exhaled slowly.

"What are you thinking?" I said, cursing under my breath.

"Sorry, didn't mean to scare you." He opened the door and climbed in. "I guess that didn't go so well?"

"Yeah, you could say that," I responded, cranking up the car. We sat in silence for a few minutes, and I guess I forgot that he wasn't really Jesus.

"Are you mad at me?" I asked.

"For what?"

"For sleeping with Jordan again today."

"Jack…" he said, drawing it out. At first I thought he was going to reach up and smack me in the back of the head, but he restrained himself. "What were you thinking, Jack?"

"I wasn't. It was so stupid."

"And you told Chloe, I assume?"

"Yes. I drove straight here afterward."

"Do you have any idea how bad that hurt her?"

"Yes! I just watched her bawl her eyes out for an hour."

"I guess your Sunday School lesson came in handy in real life then, huh?" I scowled at him and he stopped his grin from spreading. "But seriously, do you get it now?"

"Yes…ugh." I moaned, reaching out and pounding the steering wheel with both of my fists.

We sat there in silence for a moment until Yeshua spoke up again.

"I know you want to pay for your mistakes, but you can't. All we can do is take it from here and do what we can to get her back." I gritted my teeth and shook my head, trying to shake out of my funk. After a minute he said, "Hey, Jack—if you want help I'll do everything I can to help you get Chloe back, okay?"

"Really? You can like, sprinkle some kind of magic fairy dust on her and make her give me another chance?" I said, very cold and harsh.

"Not exactly," he said, a little perturbed. "But I will help you do everything you can to win her back. Deal?"

I thought about the offer for a moment. "Deal."

"What do you say we do something fun tonight, to take your mind off of things?"

"Like what?"

"I don't know. Just put this baby in drive and we'll find something to get into…"

I know, cruising Columbia with Jesus as my co-pilot. It doesn't take him long to pull my iPod out from the dash.

"You know what that thing is? I know you're from the Stone Age and all."

"Pffft," he said. "Please. Do I know what this is." He turned it on and started tapping around. "Ooh, found one." He reached down and cranked up the volume knob to my stereo.

Suddenly a country twang blurted out, and I immediately recognized it. "You've got to be kidding me. Really?"

It was "She Thinks My Tractor's Sexy" by Kenny Chesney.

I laughed so hard I started swerving. He started to sing along at the top of his lungs.

"A ha ha…I cannot believe you are singing this."

"What's wrong with Kenny Chesney?" he asked, taking a break from singing. "You know you like this song, Jack."

"Actually."

"Why do you have it on your iPod then? Busted." I shook my head and laughed.

"You are the definition of ridiculous."

"Whatever," he replied. "You're just jealous." He went back to head nodding and singing.

Next, he picked the iPod back up and started searching. "Oh snap…" he said, his face lighting up from the glare. "Brace yourself for this."

The music started and I almost fell in the floor. "The Doobie Brothers. Unbelievable." I bet you know what song it was, but just in case you don't, it was "Jesus Is Just Alright With Me." The whole time he sang he did the Egyptian pharaoh dance with his arms. Hilarious.

After the karaoke round we found ourselves sitting at Waffle House. His plan to cheer me up worked. A little.

"Glad you seem to be in a little better spirits now."

"Well, after a show like that, who wouldn't be? It's not every day you get to see 'God' sing and dance."

"True, true," he said, grinning. He stared for a second, then said, "I think you're gonna make it, Jack Bennett. You're gonna be okay." He crossed his arms over his chest and looked at me.

"I sure do hope so," I said, fidgeting with my Coke.

After we finished up our patty melts and hash browns, Glenda came over to check on us. "You fellas need anything else tonight or are you stuffed?"

"Actually," Yeshua started, "I am stuffed, but you know what, Glenda?"

"What's that?"

"Today is my birthday."

"Really? Well, happy birthday then!"

"Thank you very much, Glenda. But you know what would make my birthday?"

"What?"

"One of those pieces of chocolate pie for each of us, with maybe a little whip cream on top of them."

"Okay, I think I can handle that."

"And Glenda—one more thing…"

"Okay?"

"I want you to sing happy birthday to me."

She blushed beet red. "Oh, I couldn't possibly do that. I don't sing."

"Everyone sings Glenda, and I'm sure you have a beautiful voice. It would really make my birthday. What do you say?"

She smiled and laughed a little. "Sure. If it will make your birthday."

She put the coffee pot down and grabbed the birthday cake.

"I thought you said you were Jesus?" I whispered. "Wouldn't that mean your birthday would be December 25th?"

"Christmas? That's when people celebrate my birthday. But it's just a made up date. Nope—my real birthday is today."

"Well, then," I said, squinting. "Happy birthday to you."

"Thanks."

To our surprise, Glenda brought the cook back with her—a guy named Dave in his forties. She cleared her throat and belted out the birthday song like she was singing the national anthem at the World Series, and he accompanied her with bass. After they finished we stood to our feet and gave them a rousing standing ovation, hooting and hollering. Glenda beamed and Dave took a bow and laughed.

On the way home that night, Yeshua pulled out one last car karaoke performance. "Every Rose Has Its Thorn" by Poison. Complete with air guitar and all.

30

When I showed up at the coffee shop that Sunday morning, I was still trying to shake the soggy paralysis of a hangover from my eyes. I walked in and saw Yeshua sitting down, two bagels and coffees in front of him.

"I owed you breakfast since we were busy last week and didn't make it."

"Thanks, I appreciate that," I said, sitting down on the booth side.

"So how have you been the rest of the week, Jack?" He looked at me like he was genuinely concerned. I returned the glance but said nothing for a moment. Still hazy. "Another rough night last night?"

"You could say that," I said. "Are you going to yell at me for drinking? I assume alcohol is against your rules."

"Not at all," he responded, catching me off guard a little. "Have you never read the Bible?"

"The people at my uncle's church," I said, "always said that when it said wine in the Bible that it was just talking about grape juice."

"Right..." He answered, rolling his eyes.

"Well then, next time I get out my Woodford, I'll just call you up. You can come on over and we'll have a good ole' time."

He laughed a little at that. "I don't have any troubles to drown like you do, Jack. And it should be clear that drinking too much is never a good thing. The Bible does talk about not abusing alcohol. And some people have no business drinking because they can't handle it responsibly. Alcohol is just like most anything else, created for good and then abused and distorted by humanity in a thousand different ways. It's really sad to be honest, that everything is abused so much. And that so many people are so unhappy that they have to abuse substances just to get by in life."

"Welcome to earth," I said. "Glad you could pull up a chair and join us."

He just looked at me for a moment, but said nothing. We sat in silence for a few minutes and ate. Finally, I broke the silence.

"If you are really Jesus, why don't you have holes in your hands?" I felt like if I was a good enough sport to keep playing along with his ruse, I could at least have fun with it. We both looked down at his leathery brown hands perched on the table.

"The human body is a remarkable thing, Jack. Wounds heal." I just stared at him for a moment, but he didn't seem taken aback. After picking up his bagel to finish the last bite, he said, "Eat quickly if you can. We're running late and we need to get going."

"Where are we going today?"

"To church," he responded.

"What church?"

"*That* church." He looked at me and winked. I knew what church he was talking about, and I couldn't help but smile.

"They're just gonna kick you out again."

"We'll see about that."

I didn't really think much about our little conversation about alcohol that morning to be honest. But now that I think about it, I remember when I saw a friend in college go through DT's at the hospital. Have you ever seen anyone go through that? It's terrifying. My friend was small, but he still had to be strapped to the bed and had five security guards holding him down. Five. Alcohol owned my friend.

If you've ever seen it, you understand what I'm saying. I've thought before about how we abuse substances—about how I abuse substances. I understand that this is nothing new and has been going on for millennia. But what does it mean? Sometimes I would get plastered when things were bad, like that week after talking to Chloe. But sometimes it would be for no apparent reason at all. I would just be sitting there, and all of a sudden I would just have this urge to go get out my good Scotch. It felt like an escape, but I didn't know what I was running from. Boredom?

What does that even mean, that we need to escape? That we have this urge to alter reality, to transfer to a different existence, even if it is a clear and fleeting fake? For me, I don't know what else it could mean than that I am so utterly unhappy with life that I would rather subside in a state of intoxication for a while so I wouldn't have to think about it.

There is something about alcohol in particular that intrigues me when I think about this. If you use pills, it's just take and swallow—but there is something about alcohol, the way you can turn up the glass and feel it burning your throat and filling your stomach as it goes down. There is something natural about it that feels right when you feel that pain. Do you know what I mean? It's like this void or deficiency is a thirst, and it seems so right to pick up a bottle and gulp. It feels like it is going to help. But it doesn't. Or it does, if you consider numbness a success, and you don't mind the rage coming back with fury the next day.

31

Get this: on the way to the church that morning, a car driving perpendicular to us doesn't stop at a stop sign in time and almost, I mean *almost* plows into us on Yeshua's side. It's one of those things where you're half sure you're going to die. But the car stops just in time and I swerve to the left to avoid it. But it freaks Yeshua out so bad—he gives a little yelp and I could swear—I promise you, this is true—he reaches up and gives the finger to the person in the other car. I immediately bust out laughing—perhaps half out of relief that we are still alive—and mutter something about not believing Jesus would flip someone off. He pretends not to hear me and makes some comment about having the whole situation under control, but I know what I saw.

I saw "Jesus" give a guy the finger.

I mean, it happens to the best of us. We all lose our cool.

So at the church, there were maybe twenty-five cars in the parking lot, a high-attendance Sunday, I presumed. I could hear piano music and faint voices escaping through the doors as we walked up. I could just imagine Yeshua's anger starting to rise. Kicking a homeless man out of church? Did they not realize Jesus was a homeless man when he lived here on earth 2,000 years ago?

He sat down on the top step, so I did the same thing. "Are we not going in?" I asked.

"Not quite yet. Let's sit out here and talk a bit first."

"You planning our grand entrance?" I asked, smiling. "I like your style." He laughed. They were still singing, and I felt the need to tell him something. "Hey, just so you know—I am totally fine with going wherever with you and watching you straighten people out, especially if it is as funny as last week was. But I don't want you to waste your time if you think I'm going to one day go to a church and be all religious or something, because that's not going to happen. Maybe you're trying to prove to me that Jesus is cool, whatever that means. But beyond that I don't care about Christians or church or anything of the like, so don't expect me to ever get involved in any of that because I want nothing to do with it."

He said nothing for a moment, and looked away, thinking. Finally, he spoke: "What if I told you that it doesn't work like that?"

"What doesn't work like what?" I asked, genuinely confused.

"You don't get to pick me and not pick the church."

"I'd say you are crazy, because even if you are worth picking, they aren't. We've already discussed this…"

"Let's try this another way, Jack," he said. "How many people do you know that have had Jesus show up and talk to them individually?"

"Including me?"

"Yes, including you."

"One."

"One," he repeated. "How many people are on the planet?"

"Somewhere around six billion, last time I heard."

"What do you think that means?" he asked.

"It means I'm awesome…" I said, grinning and plucking my shirt out. "I must be something special."

"Hardly," he said. "It means that this is not the way things work. I don't make it a habit of showing up magically to people, and that's because the church is the plan for displaying me to the world. That's plan A and there is no plan B."

"Well, you might want to throw a creativity meeting together and figure out a plan B, because plan A isn't working too well, at least in America."

"You aren't getting what I'm saying. There will never be a plan B. There are a lot of things wrong with the church in America, and there are a lot of impostors that make things worse, like we talked about last week. But the church is still the plan." I just raised my eyebrows and cocked my head a little. He went on, "If you experienced a healthy, biblical church you would be overwhelmed at how beautiful it is, and how clearly you can see me through it."

"Do those exist?" I asked. "I've never seen one."

"There is no perfect church. But there are healthy churches, just like there are unhealthy churches. Unfortunately, it's just the unhealthy churches that you see more often."

"Okay. I still don't see what this means. Since I've never seen a 'healthy' church"—(I put up my quoting fingers)—"it's hard for me to believe that they exist. And still I don't think I'd want anything to do with it to be honest."

"I'm going to ask you to trust me then, Jack. I'm asking you to trust me that if, or when, you experience my gospel through a community of my followers, it will be so meaningful that it will shake you to your core. I'm asking you for you, because I'm not going to be around forever. And I'm asking you for the sake of everyone else in the world, because if they experience me, it is going to be through other believers. If churches worked like they are supposed to, then there would be no need for me to show up and talk to you, because you would see me clearly through the church —there would be no reason for people in this country to turn away from me because of what they see in Christianity. So let's talk about the problem—about what's gone wrong and how it should be. I can't make you care about it, but will you at least hear me out?"

I shuffled a bit, the concrete step starting to hurt my butt. "Sure. I guess you've earned that at least."

He smiled a bit. "Well, thank you. It's such a privilege to be obliged with your presence."

32

We slipped in the back while they were still singing a hymn and sat down on the empty back pew—unnoticed, it seemed. I kept wondering whether someone was going to come say something to the raggedy dressed man they had kicked out two weeks ago, or if they were going to leave him alone since he was with me and I looked more "presentable." We sat down with the rest of the congregation after the hymn, and it came time for the offering. A bushy haired lady played an upbeat tune on the piano and a few men came around passing golden plates down the aisles. When the spry old man on our side got to me, he reached right over Yeshua, who was sitting on the end of the row, and handed the plate to me. I reached up and slowly took the plate, while giving him a look, instantly becoming livid that he would disgrace my friend like that.

Before I could even turn to pass the plate to the other usher, however, Yeshua whispered in my ear. "Don't worry about it." He grinned wide and whispered again, "We're just gonna have a chat about some stuff. But for now just sit back and enjoy."

Enjoy? Enjoy my ass. I hadn't been in a church in over a decade for anything save funerals and weddings, and I tried to avoid as many of those as I could. The place gave me chills.

The preacher started up his sermon when the offering was over. He was a bit dry and didn't yell as much as he could have, which made me happy. I tried to listen as intently as possible, hard as it was, in case what he was saying had something to do with what Yeshua wanted to talk about. Really though, I was just hoping he would do or say something stupid so Yeshua would go all Randy Savage like he did last week. Now that was entertainment.

The main thrust of his message was about how people should behave and how they shouldn't. "People ought to be ashamed of themselves who run around and act a fool...blah blah blah...we ain't supposed to do that as Christians—that's despicable." He went on and on with a list of do's and don'ts for Christians and had stern words for anyone who got out of line.

"Christians don't go to places like that!" He kept pounding his drum like it was the only one he had. Something in his voice made it seem as though he thought the people needed some convincing.

"So what do you think of the sermon, Jack?" Yeshua broke the silence, and I was glad to have something else to listen to. I looked over to him and rolled my eyes, trying to say, "I think I've heard this one before."

"What if I told you that religion was one of the main things that keep people away from me?"

"Aren't you the founder of a major religion?" I whispered back.

"Yes, I am," he responded. "I don't necessarily mean it that way—I know Christianity is one of the world's major religions. What I'm talking about is the premise behind religion. Most people in the world believe there is a higher being who created all the majesty the world revolves in. And based on the shared moral law that permeates creation most will admit that something has gone terribly wrong. Things are fractured, broken. The machine is not running the way it seems to have been designed to.

"Because of the sin that has torn people's lives and this world apart, you can understand that something is wrong and, because of the darkness in your own hearts that you all know too well, you can understand why there would be a relational divide between you and the benevolent creator that made all of this. Many religions share these ideas. But where it goes from there is the clincher, because what question does this scenario create? The question is: 'What do I do to be right with God again?'"

102

He paused for a moment to let things sink in.

Some blue-haired lady coughed really loud, and I turned to see she was looking straight at us. Yeshua shot her a look and continued his speech.

"That's the question, and there are many answers from a thousand different religions. Do these things. Say these prayers. Go to this place and do this pilgrimage. Ad infinitum. So religion, or the premise behind it, becomes all about what you can do to make things right, to get back to peace with God and the world. But do you know what makes Christianity's answer to that question different from all other religions?" To be honest I didn't know. I remembered hearing some catchy sayings, or maybe bumper stickers, about how Christianity stood out, but I couldn't remember any.

"It's different because Christianity's answer to that question is…nothing. In and of yourself there is absolutely nothing you can do about it—nothing to make things right."

"That's kind of anticlimactic and hopeless, huh?" I asked.

"Hopeless! Hopeless? No, it's the farthest thing from it! Tell me this Jack, you have been cheating on your wife for months. Sleeping with another woman when you promised to be faithful to Chloe till death do you part. What can you do to make up for that?" He never seems to stray from making things personal, does he? "What can you do to make it right? How sweet can you be to her? How good of a husband can you be for the rest of your life? How many flowers would it take? How many love notes and boxes of chocolate?"

I only shook my head, stating the obvious answer he was getting at.

There was nothing in the universe I could do to take it back and make things right.

"Nothing. Absolutely nothing you could ever do would take away the pain and scars left by your affair and repair the rift in your relationship. What is your only hope to be restored to her?"

I sat and thought for a moment. The only answer was for her to have mercy. To be forgiven and restored to her even though I didn't deserve it.

"Grace! Unmerited, undeserved grace. That she would look at you despite your sins against her, and choose not to hold them against you—canceling the record of wrong that is rightfully yours. That she would take the pain she could rightfully inflict on you and absorb it herself. That's your only hope. It would be inane for you to think that anything else—any amount of good behavior or special acts on your behalf, could do anything to restore your marriage without her grace and forgiveness." No need arguing with him there.

"This is what sets my gospel apart from any other religion."

Right then the preacher stopped talking and looked to the back, straight at us. "Excuse me," he said loudly, directing his attention to Yeshua. "Do you have something to say?"

33

"Because if not, I'm going to ask you to either be quiet or leave," he continued. My heart thumped.

Yeshua stood up straight and crossed his arms over his chest. "You're not going to have me kicked out like you did a few weeks ago?"

"I'm not asking for trouble sir," the preacher responded. "But we are trying to have a worship service here and I am asking you not to disturb us."

Yeshua smiled. "What if I told you something really ironic? What if I told you that I was Jesus, whom you claim to worship? That would raise all kinds of interesting questions, wouldn't it?"

"Please spare us your nonsense," the preacher responded. "James, will you please escort this man outside?" He turned to a big man in a suit who was already walking our way.

Yeshua was not a very large man, but he stood there like an oak, and I stood up beside him. When James got close enough, Yeshua looked up at him and said, "James, if you know what's good for you, you will turn around and sit down." There were only four other men there, and none of them looked much like the fighting type. James looked over at me, a bit bigger than him, and I said, "You heard him." That place was so tense you could taste it. It tasted like honey to me.

All of a sudden Yeshua looked around at the congregation and said, "Everyone get out your Bibles. Turn to Luke 18 and follow along with the story." Then, he took a few steps to the door of the church and opened it. Two men came in, one on each side of James and at that point he decided that he was outnumbered and sat down. They didn't stop and walked straight for the front of the church.

The first man was dressed ornately, clean and proper looking, with a fancy looking hat kind of thing on his head and a ritzy, ugly robe on. The second one looked much more simple, and he dropped to his knees and sat there looking at the floor. I was taken aback to say the least. Who were these men?

The first suddenly raised his head in the air, standing tall, and prayed: "God, I thank you that I am not like other men, extortioners, unjust, adulterers, or even like this tax collector. I fast twice a week; I gives tithes of all that I get." He looked proud and arrogant, and had the attitude of many religious people that I had met. Then, the second man, the tax collector I presume, stood up, but in a different way—more humbly—and wouldn't even lift his eyes upward. He began to beat his chest with his fists, and screamed, "God, be merciful to me, a sinner!" Something about his scream made chills go down my spine, and probably everyone else in the room too.

Yeshua walked over to the tax collector, who just stood looking down, tears falling from his eyes. He looked around the room, then at me. "Out of these two, this man is the one who walks away justified. He is the one who understands the gospel. He gets the fact that he is a sinner, completely helpless and unable to do anything about his sin on his own. His only hope is in the undeserved grace of God. So he reaches out in faith to let my grace do what he could never do for himself. Do you see it? The utter helplessness in his voice that points him to my grace?"

I nodded.

"Do you think this guy would ever kick a homeless guy out of church?" He looked around at the rest of the attendees, white as ghosts. I nodded my head no. "Why?" he asked.

"Because he knows he is no better," I said.

"Exactly!" he said. "He knows he is no better. He has a correct estimate of himself outside of my grace, and that precludes any boasting or condescension. And that awareness will only deepen as he grows in his faith."

"But what about this guy?" he asked, pointing to the Pharisee, still standing there with his eyes open, chest stuck out.

"That's the guy who kicks homeless people out of churches," I said. "He looks a lot like the angry, judgmental, right-wing finger pointers."

Yeshua nodded, going on. "His spirit is an attitude of self-righteousness that finds its value from comparing himself to other people who seem worse off. That's the demeanor of *religion*. That's the attitude that you see in so many religious people in your culture that are finding their righteousness in themselves, that seems so disgusting to you—because it *is* disgusting. That pride is more abhorrent to me than any outward immorality—that's why if you read the Gospels you will see that I reserved my harshest words for the religious people of that day, just like this offensive parable that I told. That's the attitude that gets homeless people kicked out of churches. Look around this room, Jack. What do you see?"

I surveyed the people sitting in the church. Everyone was scared out of their minds, but I could still see their demeanor through the fear. There were a few people who seemed to have the gentler spirit of the tax collector, but I could tell even they were very confused. "I see a bunch of Pharisees, I guess." And I think they were starting to think that he really was Jesus.

"The religious people in this room," Yeshua went on, "don't really believe the gospel, but turn my message into a twisted kind of moralism that does not and cannot save from anything. These people are essentially trying to bargain with God. They are coming and saying, 'Okay, I'll do this, this, and this for you, and then you give me what I want.'

"The trouble is, there's no such thing as bargaining with God. You cannot pay for or earn salvation in any way—it is not for sale. Trying to buy it is a hopeless cause. The gospel is found in coming to God with gloriously empty hands that despair of anything they could possibly bring to the table. That's the only place that true hope and salvation is found. And my father longs...he loves to freely give away what you cannot earn. Are you starting to see the difference?"

I nodded a bit, thinking I was seeing the difference. He looked around at the crowd to make sure they were still listening. Like they could do anything else! At this point also, the two men, whoever they were, walked out of the church and shut the door behind them. I guess their job was finished.

"I hope you see the despair of religion." He spoke to them with a stern kindness in his voice. "And I am not fooled. I know what you do when no one is watching." I thought one man, shirt and tie sitting on the front row, was going to faint at that. Evidently he had a lot of secrets.

"And even if you don't have a lot of outward sin, and you've been able to clean yourselves up a bit over the years, your prideful, arrogant heart is more detestable to God than anything you could ever do on the outside. It is a stench in God's nostrils.

"But the gospel is still true, though many of you have forgotten it or never really understood it. You bring nothing to the bargaining table. The gospel is not 'you do,' but 'Jesus did'. You can't clean yourself up and make yourself acceptable to God, but you can, like the tax collector, beat your chest and cry out to God in faith to save you. And he will. Gladly. Most of you need to repent of your religion and believe the gospel that humbles you and frees you from the chains of self-righteousness. Then you will have nothing to boast in, and this good news will rob you of your sense of superiority over others. Then, you will be a much better picture of me to a world that desperately needs to see it."

I looked around the room at the audience. Some were crying, and some were just still in shock. Yeshua began to walk out and I followed, and at the back of the church he turned around to say one last thing: "Don't you dare go anywhere. Stay here as long as you need to and repent of your righteousness."

With that, we turned around and left.

34

Before he left that Sunday he asked me if I wanted to meet him for dinner at The Whig.

"You know about The Whig?" I asked, genuinely surprised.

"Of course I know about The Whig," he said.

I never would have expected "Jesus" to suggest such a hole-in-the-wall bar (even in light of their incredible burgers and fries). I've seen families walk in to The Whig, only to turn around and walk right back out. It is in the basement of the ABC News station on Main Street near the State House, and not a lot of people really know about it. It's a dingy, ironically pretentious place that might as well be the unofficial hipster hang-out of Columbia (although I might just have made it official). We'll have to go there sometime if you want. If you don't already go there, that is. I just haven't seen you there. Maybe you already love it as much as I do.

So when I got there that night he was already there, sitting in the back booth, right next to those three pictures of creepy-looking men, the tiny chandelier, and the huge mounted fish with the birthday hat on.

We talked about how awesome the burgers were for a minute and then argued over whether the sweet potato fries or the regular fries were better. We ended up in a draw because both of them are *amazing*, as you might well know. Then he went to place our order at the bar and brought us both back an oatmeal stout draft.

"Your favorite, right?" he asked.

"Yes," I said, taking my first sip. "Though it's still a bit weird that I'm drinking a beer with Jesus."

"Well, get used to it," he said, and raised his glass to clink against mine.

"So when are you gonna drop this whole Jesus act and tell me who you really are? If I get you drunk enough tonight will you spill the beans?"

He smiled and put his beer down. "How many times do I have to tell you Jack? It's not an act. And good luck getting me drunk. Not gonna happen."

"All right, fair enough," I said. "I'll keep playing along." About that time this song came on—blaring out of the speaker right behind us—some woman singing about "Sweet Handsome Jesus" and why wouldn't he listen and answer her prayers or something like that. It was really funny and he made a big deal out of it of course, said that it proved he was Jesus. I wish I could find the song—I've tried to Google it and can't find it anywhere.

"Speaking of a handsome Jesus," I said, "I heard somewhere that the Bible says you were ugly? And I have to admit, you don't look anything like that picture on the cover of Time Magazine I saw."

"Well, ugly is in the eye of the beholder Jack. But you know because you're sitting here that I'm a ten." He gave me his best model pose and put his chin on his hand and I laughed.

I said he was a four and a half, maybe, and he said no way. Our burgers came out not long afterward, and we ate.

Yeshua mumbled after chewing a few bites, "You know why God made food taste so good Jack?"

"Because he likes good food?"

"Well, yeah," he said, wiping his face with a napkin. "And, because he wants to remind you that he is good." He took another bite and then looked up at me. "Why do you spend your money for that which is not bread, and your labor for that which does not satisfy? Listen diligently to me, and eat what is good, and delight yourselves in rich food."

"What is that, some kind of weird poem you wrote?"

"Well, not exactly. That's Isaiah 55. One of my favorite scriptures. Comes right after, 'Come, everyone who thirsts, come to the waters; and he who has no money, come, buy and eat!'"

"Interesting," I said. "So God runs a restaurant. Don't think I've been there."

"Not quite," he said. "It's just a passage that pretty much sums up your life—that God is the only source of true satisfaction, and you've been spending your money on things that don't satisfy."

"Ouch," I said, grabbing my chest and pretending to hurt. "You go straight for the jugular don't you?"

"The truth has to make you miserable before it can set you free." He winked at me and took a sip of his beer. I didn't respond, so after a moment he continued. "Idolatry, Jack, is devotion to anything else besides God—looking to any created thing for the source of life, value, satisfaction and peace that can only be found in the creator. I'm sure you've heard the old quote about how a man knocking on the door of a brothel is really looking for God."

I interjected and very politely said that if he told me I had a God-shaped hole in my heart I was going to throw up in my mouth. He laughed and promised me that he wouldn't say that.

"Your life shows what you worship like a billboard. What you spend time and money on, what you pay attention to, what you devote yourself to and find important or valuable. Take your life, for example. Early on, you idolized sports. They were your life and your functional savior—as long as you could excel at sports you'd be okay. Because you weren't big enough to play at the next level, your sports idol let you down. In college your functional saviors were girls, fun, and popularity, but they all eventually ran out of steam. You met Chloe and pursued your satisfaction in her—but what happens when people idolize one another is that they suck the life out of one another. Idolizing a person is destroying them, because there is no way any person can carry that load—to be the source of another's life and well being. No human can fully satisfy another. It's too much to handle. Chloe couldn't give you what you were looking for, so you turned to worship success and importance through work. When that failed you, you found Jordan. It's really

111

that simple. Besides the fact that along the way you've toyed with pills to numb the pain of functional saviors that failed you."

I stared blankly at him.

"One theologian said it this way: 'Human history is the long terrible story of man trying to find something other than God which will make him happy.'"

I interrupted him. "All this talk about idolatry," I said, "to be honest with you, it kind of sounds embarrassing. Very primitive and irrelevant."

He smirked and wiped his mouth with his napkin. "Primitive and irrelevant, huh?" he said. "In reality, Jack, it's more sophisticated than you realize. It integrates intellectual, spiritual, behavioral, psychological, cultural, and social categories. And most of what I've mentioned are just typical surface idols. You're not ready for what happens when you get down to the deep source idols that fuel everything else. Deep idols like control. Approval. Comfort. Attention. Power. Acceptance. Those are pretty much the driving force of every human being—the things beneath much of human behavior and interaction. Humans are idol factories, churning out modern golden calves erected to find meaning, power and pleasure apart from God."

I tried to act uninterested as I kept eating my burger. But it didn't stop him from talking.

"Do you ever feel like a slave to your impulses Jack?" I shook my head no, but it was a lie. That question thumped my insides somehow. "Like when your heart leaps at something," he said, "like when it leapt at Jordan and convinced you that if you just had her you'd be happy, you'd be okay. But as time goes by you learn that your impulses don't know any more about what you really want than you do."

I didn't say anything, just looked at him.

"Broken people bowing down to broken gods that can't save. Idol after idol fails, but you keep trading one for another, because however disappointing, you hold onto something—because the heart revolts against its own emptiness. But the way out of idolatry, Jack, is repentance and worship. You have to learn that God is truly better than any idol—that Jesus is the good life you're looking for and chasing after."

"Okay," I said, interrupting. "I see what's going on here, and I'm not buying this."

"What's going on here?"

"You are exploiting the basic human condition. Sure, people have a longing for transcendence, for purpose and community. But you're just turning this whole God thing into a product that meets those needs. Everyone is trying to sell us something and you are just another vendor in the line. I know people thirst for transcendence, but a doorknob can fill that need."

"You really want to bow down and worship a piece of brass?" He looked amused, but I could have sworn he was getting uncomfortable with this train of thought.

"Okay, bad example," I said, thinking. "I could start a soup kitchen and meet those same needs. Transcendence…helping others. Purpose…feeding the hungry. Community…doing it with other people. People just use God as a crutch—as some smiling, distant, vague deity to give them a self-esteem boost."

"Jack, you are a smart guy. I'll admit that a soup kitchen would be a more fulfilling thing to worship than a doorknob, but it would still end in misery. A lot of times it's even easier to think that good things like soup kitchens can satisfy our deepest needs and hopes, but they can't. Lots of things have shadows of life in them because God uses them to point to himself. But none of them— none of them can ever be the source of life. There is no breath in them. It's like a man dying of thirst drinking water from a thimble." I smirked at him, shook my head, and took a sip of my beer.

Then he looked up at me and said, "For instance—sex is fun, isn't it Jack?" I nodded. "But," he went on, "have you ever noticed that even in the short-lived ecstasy that sex brings, that you hit a ceiling?"

I squinted my eyes at him. "No, I'm afraid I've never hit a ceiling while having sex. You must be a wild man."

He laughed at me. "You know that's not what I mean," he said. "I mean a ceiling, like," he put his left hand out and then his right below it, and started raising his right hand to smack the other. "Like when you feel like you should be able to go farther, to get more pleasure and fulfillment from this act, but you can't. It just stops short. It's over." He paused for a moment and looked my way. After I didn't respond, he said, "How completely satisfying it must be to turn from your innumerable limitations to a God that has none. To find that he is beyond all of the ceilings you hit."

I just took another bite and didn't answer him, so he did the same. After chewing for a bit, he sat back and said, "Anyway, what you were trying to argue earlier is that what you worship doesn't matter, but you've already proven with your life that it does."

My mind was spinning trying to formulate a response, but instead it decided to change directions. "You know, that's another thing I really don't like about your God. Always glory-hungry, doing everything for his own fame, demanding that people worship him and glorify his name or whatever. Sounds like some giant, insecure megalomaniac in the sky who needs us fledgling humans to raise our hands in adoration to boost *his* self-esteem. It's rather unappealing."

He leaned toward me over the table and looked rather serious. "You think God really needs your worship? You think he is somehow lacking and could really be served by human hands, that he is a nervous middle school boy waiting by the phone, biting his nails and praying you'll call because he needs your approval and will just be crushed if he doesn't get it?"

"Well, yeah, it kind of sounds like it."

He smiled and sat back. "Oh, Jack. God doesn't *need* anything from you, or from anyone else for that matter. He rightfully deserves your glory but he doesn't need it. He is completely sufficient in and of himself." He twisted his beer on the table and bored his eyes into mine. "What if he actually wants to include you in the joy that he already exists in? What if his glory leads to your joy—what if it's the only thing that leads to your joy?"

"What leads to my joy," I said, leaning his way and putting my hand over a very full stomach, "is a delicious burger and a beer."

He grinned at me and sat back. "I'll just tell you this, Jack. Psalm 16 says that the sorrows of those who run after other gods will only multiply. Just hold on to that sentence in your mind and see if it doesn't describe your life as you grow older."

I smiled back at him. "You never run out of those little sayings, do you? I'll admit, they are more interesting than most of the ones I've heard."

"Some wandered in desert wastes, finding no way to a city to dwell in; hungry and thirsty, their soul fainted within them...for he satisfies the longing soul, and the hungry soul he fills with good things," he said. "Psalm 107."

"Could be," I said, nodding my head. "Or it could be the naïve soul he fills with nonsense..."

"I guess we'll just have to wait and see, huh? Only time will tell if you are the hungry soul who finds true food, or the naïve soul who keeps filling itself with nonsense."

"Nah," I shook my head. "I already know you're a fake. You're probably just a figment of my imagination." He kicked my shin under the table and asked me if that was fake, so I kicked him back and said yeah, that was too.

"I hate to break this to you, Mr. Yeshua, but I am a middle-class, all-American resident of the US of A, and that means if I want you to be a fake and your God to be the source of nothing, then that's that and there's nothing you can do about it. I am the ultimate arbiter of truth in my own little universe. Sorry, but there's nothing you can do about that."

"Yikes," he said, grimacing. "If that were only a joke it would be funny. But that pretty much nails it on the head. A bunch of self-righteous rich people judging God—setting themselves up as their own deity. It's quite nauseating. "

"Well," I said, "welcome to our 'Be Your Own Deity Club'. Pull up a chair and join us, it's nice here." I paused and reached to grab my keys. "Actually, on second thought, I guess you're already a member. You might even be president..."

35

You know what makes me sad, and sometimes a little angry? People like that guy who just walked in, huffing and puffing and all in a hurry, typing away on his smart phone and rolling his eyes. People like that who seem to have lost all of their sense of wonder at this world. People who are over it, constantly unimpressed and ungrateful.

I don't know if you saw it, but a bunch of years ago there was an interview on Conan (you know, when he was on a network) with a comedian named Louis C.K. I think it's called "Everything's Amazing and Nobody's Happy" on YouTube. He talks about cell phones, and how people get so frustrated with their smart phones taking a few seconds to get to the Internet, and then he screams and goes, "Give it a second! It's going to SPACE! Can you give it a second to get back from SPACE?" (Sorry for the hypocrisy but I have to use all caps to capture his tone!)

Then he talks about people complaining about flight delays and goes, "Oh really…what happened next? Did you fly through the air, incredibly? Like a bird? Did you partake in the miracle of human flight, you non-contributing zero? You're FLYING! It's amazing! You're sitting in a chair IN THE SKY!"

It's funny because it's true.

I think about this sometimes when I am outside at night, and it's one of those nights where the moon just strikes me. It's gorgeous, isn't it? All the craters and shades, and thinking about how it rotates around us constantly. And then the fact that we have actually put human beings on that thing. That is astounding. But nobody thinks it is anymore, and elementary school kids probably smirk at the triviality of it.

And have you ever thought about the fact that the earth you stand on is just a big ball? A ball of dirt and water that somehow stays round, with crust and rock and molten lava all in the middle. It's almost comical, isn't it?

And music—don't get me started on music. We used to have this old record player in our house, the kind you had to wind up and it would play through this big metal cone of a speaker. So you put the metal needle down on this plastic, black, round thing that spins, and then somehow beautiful music comes streaming out of this other piece of metal. What? I know, I know. You could probably explain to me how it works in fifteen seconds. But I don't care. The sheer fact that it works is just magic. Go take a piece of metal and rub in on a piece of plastic and see if it erupts in a beautiful song. And if you think I am juvenile for calling that magic, then I think you are an ungrateful jackass. No offense, but it's true.

So that next Wednesday was a rough day at work, so I went to the coffee shop that night to relax. My eyes burned from looking at my laptop screen, so I closed it for a moment and closed my eyes to take a breath. My insides were still stewing from earlier that afternoon, when I had driven over to my house, worried sick about Chloe and the boys. She hadn't returned a phone call or text in two days and I started to panic. Then, I show up at the house and she acts like everything is fine, and she shoots that arrow at me, "Why are you so worried about us now, Jack?"

My blood was still crackling like a boiling pot. How dare she? Could she not see that I was really trying? Was this just her way of making things as hard as possible for me, exacting every bit of revenge she could out of it, leaving me dangling and worrying that we were finished, no matter what I do? All while I'm still paying the mortgage on the house? My mind raced a few thousand feet per second, and before long I was half convinced that I was the victim here. You know, if such and such had been different, maybe I wouldn't have turned to Jordan that way. "You don't deserve to be treated that way," the voice in my head says. Not a crazy voice…the voice that is me, somehow. Talking to me. You know what I mean. At least I hope so.

It is astonishing how quickly I can sometimes jump from self-loathing to self-righteousness.

Pile all that on top of the deadline for the article due the next day and my brain was a slushie machine, going 'round and 'round and nowhere at the same time. I couldn't even write, I was so frustrated, so I decided that I needed to go home (to Sara's) and have a beer to calm down. Something stout. After one more refill of coffee, though, because I felt like I was going to need it.

I traipsed up to the counter and paid for my refill, then over to the urns and pressed myself a full cup of Guatemalan. I turned quickly and bumped into something that felt human. My coffee almost showered them with burns in the face, but I have to say I've always had crazy reflexes. Crisis avoided.

Awkwardness, though, definitely not avoided.

"Oh, hey Jack," Jordan said, straightening up from thinking she was about to be scalded with hot coffee. "Didn't expect to see you here this late."

"Yeah, I'm working on that article due tomorrow morning. Having a really tough time with it, honestly."

"Oh, I'm sure you'll do fine."

Insert awkward silence here.

"Listen, Jordan," I said, shifting a little. "I'm sorry about everything. I didn't mean to hurt you."

"I know. No worries Jack," she replied, with a fake smile.

"Well," insert another awkward pause, "It was good seeing you."

"You too Jack…"

I started to turn to walk away.

"Jack," she said, turning me back around. "Did you tell your wife?"

"Yes, I did."

"Are things okay? You still living at home?"

"No and no."

"Oh," she said, glancing around a bit and giving me a bit of a smile. "If you want—I could help you finish the article since you are having trouble. Just as friends this time, of course. Come by?"

My heart pounded and my mind spun like that teacup ride at the fair. It seemed like a relief from a lot the frustration—a carrot dangling in front of me. The voice started again, "Yes, yes…tell her yes." But, there was another voice, saying something quite different. I promise, I'm not crazy. If I am, you are too, because I know you know what I'm talking about. It suddenly became a matter of which voice I was going to shut up and which I was going to turn the volume up on.

My mouth opened, "Maybe I'll…" *Stop.* I froze. While pronouncing the words, I glanced over to see Yeshua at the counter with his back to me, putting cream in his coffee. "Jordan, I can't. Sorry. Thanks. I hope you have a good night." With that, I walked away from her without waiting for a response and straight toward Yeshua. I just knew he was about to crush me and make me feel like the little boy that I was.

When I got right behind him, he still had not turned, so I tapped him on the shoulder. He turned, only it wasn't him. It was a Hispanic man, with a striking resemblance to Yeshua, besides being Hispanic, and shorter. His face was a little older, but his eyes were similarly kind and piercing, and I was almost taken aback at the likeness. I knew him from somewhere, but couldn't place it.

"*Hola!*" He was smiling. "You need something, friend?"

I snapped out of my daze, hoping I didn't creep him out. He stood there looking at me in ragged clothes, book bag strapped on, Braves hat backward. "No. Sorry. I thought you were… someone else."

"Whew…" he said. "I thought I was in troubles." He laughed a slow, rolling giggle at that. I instantly remembered where I knew him from.

"Oh no," I said. "No troubles here. What is your name?"

"Luis. What is your name?"

"Jack."

"Nice to meet you, Jack."

He shook my hand with a surprisingly tight grip for a man of his size.

"Those hands look like they're no stranger to hard work."

"Oh yee-us. I am a very hard worker. You need some work?"

"Oh, no…well um, not really. I'm a writer, so I don't do much physical labor. I was just commenting on your strong grip."

"Oh, I see. Sorry." he said, eyes clearly disappointed. My heart kind of broke for him. And he just got me out of what could have been a disaster.

"Well, it was nice to meet you, Jack." He shook my hand again and started to walk away.

"Wait, Luis. Are you good with building stuff? With wood?"

His eyes perked up. "Ooh yeah. I can build anything!"

I turned some things over in my brain. "What are you doing on Saturday?"

36

He is not someone you easily forget.

I had never met him, but had sat next to him at the same coffee shop the past summer. It was a really hot day, and I was there working on my computer, earphones in. He sat at the table next to me with a cup of water—a homeless man taking a brief reprieve from the weather, I assumed. He seemed to be talking to himself, so I paused my music and listened in a bit. Do you ever do that? Earphones can be quite helpful when you need them to be.

I couldn't really make out what he was saying. Most of it was in Spanish, but he seemed so happy and quirky that I just continued to listen, pretending to work. Sometimes he just hummed. His cell phone vibrated in his pocket, interrupting the humming, and he made a big deal out of getting it out, like he was really excited to talk to whoever it was. I was sitting there with my laptop, so I started writing it all down. Not eavesdropping, right? Just practicing transcribing.

"*Hola*! Hey buddy! How you been? *No mucho, no mucho*. I still walking and walking, you know?" I love trying to figure out conversations from only hearing one side. "Pretty good, *ese*, pretty good... no. No work today. I still trying, but it doesn't look good, you know. It's okay though—I had a little yesterday. And I have some, I think, on Friday. Probly I do, probly I don't. We'll see. Nah, I don't like work—it's too hard!"

Then, "All right, all right," he said in his drawn-out way.

"Oh yeah buddy, I'm fine," he went on.

"We got plenty food. No, I got plenty—almost too much!" he said, laughing. "I be fine, buddy. God is good, he provides. I know. I appreciate it, for real. Thank you. Ooh, yeah. I be there. I see you tomorrow night buddy. Have a good night, and tell your wife I say, 'Hi'. And tell that, how you say, little thing, I say 'Ruff ruff.'" He laughed.

"Bye," he said, closing the phone and tucking it back into his pants pocket. Then he looked at his watch. It was almost 4:00. He rubbed his stomach and said to himself, "I'm hungry." Then he got his wallet from his back pocket, opening it to reveal a solitary dollar. "There will be dinner tomorrow night…I want dinner tonight, or breakfast tomorrow?" He seemed to have a light-bulb moment, laughed and grinned from ear to ear. He got up, grabbed his book bag, and murmured, "Thanks, God," as he half-skipped out the door.

And here he was again.

Crap—

You just scared me really bad. Suddenly I looked up and you were gone and I thought you had left and I was going to have to pull something really awkward. But you were just in the restroom. Whew.

37

That Thursday night Sara got home from work early, and I was sitting in the living room watching TV. Exciting life, huh?

"Hey honey, I'm home," she said as she walked in.

"Welcome, pull up a chair. There are some wonderfully staged reality shows on that will make you dumber than you were before you sat down."

"Wonderful, just what I'm in the mood for." She put her purse down and flopped down on the couch.

"Work was fantastic, I presume?"

"Always," she said smiling, not opening her eyes. I stared at her for a moment while she had her eyes closed. She was so sweet and gorgeous, just like she always had been. I wish we could have been closer through the years, though it makes sense why we weren't.

"Do you have any Tylenol?" I asked. "Reality TV gives me a headache."

"Top cabinet, left-hand side of the sink."

"Thanks."

I got up and walked over to the kitchen and started opening up cabinets. I froze as I opened up the second one, still looking for the Tylenol. There were over a dozen bottles of prescription pills, and then more that were still prescription but were in bottles that were bought from somewhere other than the pharmacy. I looked through them for a minute because Sara couldn't see me from where she was sitting. I cursed under my breath, then grabbed a few of the bottles and walked over to where Sara could see me. "Sara—what are these?"

She looked up at me. "Put those back, Jack. It's none of your business. I said you could live here, not be my daddy and rummage through my stuff." She closed her eyes again.

"Sara I thought you weren't using anymore. I thought you were doing better. What else are you using?"

"Nothing, Jack." She was never a good liar. "I'm fine. Leave me alone and put those back where you found them. I don't take them anymore—just haven't cleaned out my cabinets in a long time." She was getting angry, so I obliged and sat back down on the couch. There was an awkward silence and the TV blared some nonsense commercials.

"Sara, how are you doing, for real?" I asked, breaking the silence.

"Peachy, Jack. Never been better. How about you?"

I shook my head at her and said nothing for a bit. "I'm serious, Sara. Please talk to me and tell me what's going on."

"Talk to you about what, Jack?" She got up and walked into the kitchen to get a glass of water. "About all my problems and hang-ups? What do you want me to say about them? You want to be my counselor?"

"I'm just trying to help, Sara."

"If you want to help, change the channel."

"Okay." I started flipping through the channels.

"I actually got a Netflix in the mail today—let's watch that. It's been a long day."

It wasn't long into the movie before Sara had fallen asleep. When I was sure she was out, I got a piece of paper out and went into the kitchen to count all of the pills in each bottle.

That night I ended up having to borrow one of Sara's sleeping pills to get to sleep.

38

The next night I was at the apartment alone because Sara was working, and the next thing I know, Yeshua's at the door with takeout Chinese from this dumpy place up the street and we ate and relaxed for a bit. I was really down because of all the stuff with Sara and of course, my wrecking ball of a life. I missed Chloe and I missed my boys.

I talked to him about it a little, but mostly just wanted to pout and sulk, so that's basically what I did.

But then he asked if I had a guitar, and I told him no, but that Sara did I thought. I went in her room, found it and brought it back to him. I plopped down on the couch again and he started picking and tuning.

"I'm gonna show you what I like to do to cheer up when I'm sad," he said.

"Please, go ahead," I said, dripping with sarcasm. "Serenade me—that will surely cure all of my problems."

"No—not a serenade," he said. "A sing-a-long. A *Garth Brooks* sing-a-long."

I rolled my eyes and mumbled something about him being ridiculous.

"It doesn't work unless you sing along," he said. "And I know you love Garth Brooks. Don't lie to me—you're from South Carolina."

"Of course I love Garth Brooks," I said. "I grew up on Double Live. But let's be honest—there's no way you're pulling off that on the guitar. I can already tell you're a beginner. You're certainly no Garth Brooks…"

"Oh, really?" he said, then immediately began playing a few chords that I recognized. "How about I get us started and you can join whenever you get your panties out of a wad?" I glared at him.

"I'll start with something slow to make a good transition."

He kept the rhythm going and I recognized the song—"The River". I smiled as he began singing the words, but tried to hide it. I have to be honest…it wasn't bad at all. I wouldn't say it was good, like Son of God good, but it definitely wasn't bad. About halfway through the song I started nodding my head a little, and he was encouraged, egging me to sing with him. He winked at me during the part about the good Lord being captain or something like that, and I laughed. As the song ended, he started right into the next one.

It was "The Dance," if you were wondering. I'm still pissed about it, because he knew it would get me. He just knew it. It was unfair to play that song right then, and he knew it by the time he got to the second word.

By the way, if you don't like that song for some reason, you can get out of here. If I knew you didn't like it I'd stop writing this right now and walk out. Because there's something clinically wrong with you.

I'm just playing. I wouldn't do that.

But I do love that song.

And I did start singing along, quietly at first. Then a little louder and a little louder, and at the end it was like I was at a karaoke bar with a rum and Coke in my hand raised up in the air. By the end of the song I might have had my concert lighter app on my iPhone lit, waving it in the air.

He ate it up, of course, and then launched right into the next song—"Standing Outside the Fire," and he was playing it like he was Garth himself, strutting on a Central Park stage. During the chorus I stood up on the couch and pumped my fist, yelling the words as he swayed back and forth strumming, and then during the drum part I sat down and beat on the coffee table. At least I did until the music instantly stopped and I was drumming and singing myself. I looked up to see Yeshua's face white as a ghost. Sara stood in the doorway, head tilted with squinty eyes. "Jack?" was all she could manage to say.

"Hey, Sara," I said, getting up very quickly to go over to her. I was so embarrassed. She wasn't supposed to be home until ten. "Sorry, we were just having a little sing-a-long."

She looked at both of us like we were playing one of those weird role-playing games in the park with fake swords. "Yeah, I can see that," she said. Then her eyes rested on Yeshua.

"Sorry sis, I'm rude," I said. "This is my friend…um, his name is Yeshua." I couldn't think of anything else. They exchanged pleasantries and he was quite embarrassed as he took her guitar off and thanked her for letting us borrow it.

"Please, don't let me interrupt your sing-a-long," she said.

Yeshua and I laughed hesitantly and I said no, we had had enough for one night. Then Sara commented on Yeshua's name and I interjected to say it was Greek and he nodded. And she asked him where he was from and he said something about it being a long story, kind of from everywhere. I got nervous and wanted to change the subject, so I told them I had a bootleg copy of *Inception* that we could watch if they wanted to.

"I thought that wasn't out on DVD yet?" Sara asked.

"It isn't. I said bootleg."

"Oh, gotcha. Yeah. I've been wanting to see that."

"Me too," I said, getting up to get the movie. Then I stopped and smiled, looking back at Yeshua. "I guess I should check with you first, I mean—Sara, to catch you up, Yeshua is a cool guy, but he also happens to be quite the Bible-thumper, so… Yeshua, is it okay with your religious standards to watch a bootleg DVD? I don't want to offend you or anything. I mean, I know I'm a heathen and all so—"

"Jack—" he interrupted, giving me quite a look, then smiled. "Go get the movie before I punch you."

39

Saturday around lunchtime I met Luis in Five Points, then we drove to my house. I was building a playhouse for the boys' birthday and Chloe was nice enough to let me come over to work on it.

We got of the car and out came the boys, running. "Daddy, daddy!" They both jumped in my arms and I gave them bear hugs. I missed them so much, and I was glad they were too young to fully realize what was going on. They just knew they missed me.

I put them down and Luis started working his charm on them. "Hola, amigos!" He held out his hand for a high five, and both of them reached up and gave him a good one. Then he moved his hands down low to the ground, and they swung in time for him to move them and leave them whiffing. He laughed and pointed at them and they chuckled with him.

Chloe was outside by now. "Hey, Jack," she said coldly.

"Hey Chloe, good to see you. This is my friend Luis—he's going to help me work on the playhouse."

"Hi, Luis, nice to meet you." She reached out her hand without a smidge of affection.

"Nice to meet you too." He bowed a bit as he shook her hand.

"We'll just be around back working," I said.

"Okay, let me know if y'all need anything. I'll try to keep the boys out of your hair."

"No, no—by all means let them come play as much as they want. I miss them terribly."

She bit her lip at that and yelled for the boys to come to her, that they were going inside. Luis and I drove around to the back yard and I started getting out the wood and materials.

"What's going on *ese*? This is your house, right?" Luis asked, concerned.

"Yeah. It is. We are just separated for the time being, so I don't live here right now."

"Uh oh…" he said. "You in troubles." Very matter-of-fact, my new friend.

"Yeah, you could say that," I answered, not wanting to talk about it anymore. "Will you grab those bags of cement over there and bring them here?"

We worked for a little while pouring some cement for the support poles. Then Isaac and Liam shot out the back door and started chasing each other around, so I joined in the fun for a few minutes. Luis joined my team and before long we were picking them up and tickling them until they almost lost their breath. We sat them down to catch their breath and I walked over to my iPod player to change the music to some techno. It blared out and both of the boys perked up and looked at me.

"Get up and dance!"

They stood quickly, smiling, and started to jiggle and shake back and forth while I turned up the volume. I had taught them to breakdance several months back while watching some documentary on VH1. Cutest thing you could ever see.

They rolled and spun around in the grass and Isaac even tried to do a headstand. Which didn't quite work out for him. Luis and I both were laughing hysterically, when Chloe burst outside. "Boys, boys—you are getting grass stains all over your good pants!" She grabbed them gently and stood them up, wiping off their clothes while they laughed.

Before I knew it, the day was almost over. We got a good bit of the playhouse finished, but still had a long way to go. I decided to call it quits for the night. While we packed up our stuff, I noticed a red Mini Cooper in the driveway that belonged to Sharon, one of Chloe's best friends.

We walked inside to say goodbye. Sharon was perched on a stool at the bar, watching Isaac and Liam play in the living room. "Hello, Jack." She might has well have stuck a knife in me with her tone.

"Hey, Sharon. Good to see you." She turned around to face the boys. "You hanging out here tonight?"

"Yep. Watching the kids for Chloe while she goes out for a while."

"Cool. Where is she—"

"Jack." Chloe walked into the room in my favorite dress of hers, putting on her earrings. "Y'all are leaving, I guess?"

"Yeah, we were just about to head out. It's getting dark."

"Yep," she said, picking up her feet to put on her heels. Man, she was beautiful.

"You going out with some friends?" I asked, patting my pockets to make it clear we were on our way out.

"I don't think that's any of your business, Jack," Sharon piped in. I turned and gave her a nasty look, and right about then the doorbell rang. Chloe walked over to open the door.

"Donnie, hey, come on in," Chloe said. It was Donnie Clark, a guy we had gone to college with who now owned a carpet cleaning business.

I never have liked him.

"Isaac, Liam—come with me," Sharon said, getting up to grab them by the hands. "I need to show you something in your bedroom."

Donnie walked in the living room decked out in black pants and a black shirt, with a green tie. He looked like an *idiot*. All of this gel caked in his hair—I could smell his awful cologne as soon as he stepped in.

"Well, we better get going," Chloe said to us. "Luis, it was nice to meet you. Jack, have a good night."

She turned away and Donnie half-smiled and nodded at me. What kind of jackass smiles at you when he's about to walk out the door with your wife?

Have I ever told you I can be a bit of a hothead?

"Hold up a minute," I said, walking towards them. "You are going on a *date*? With this *loser*? Where did you get that cologne Donnie, the jockey lot?" He made a face at me.

"Jack, grow up. And shut up. I can do whatever I want, and yes, I am going on a date with Donnie. You can leave now."

"The hell you are—" I was really flaring up now. I hate getting like that. I turned to Donnie. "Sorry to break this to you Donnie, but you aren't going anywhere with my *wife*."

"I'm not your wife anymore, Jack. The divorce papers will be delivered to you next week." I took a step back, feeling like I'd just been punched in the stomach.

Donnie, naturally, thought it was a good time to interject. "Don't you have some whore to go screw, Jack?"

My blood is boiling even now as I think back about that moment. I reared back to take a swing at him, but Luis caught my arm behind me and held me there—he was much stronger than I expected. I stood there, red-faced, arms behind my back, four inches away from Donnie's face. He didn't flinch—putting on the tough-guy pose to try to impress Chloe.

"All right, boys," Chloe interjected. "I'm so over this pissing contest. Jack, you better get going. I'm sure you have some *work* to do."

The prick smiled at that and glanced over at Chloe. His glance took him away just long enough for me to hock a loogie right between his eyes. There was a bit of a scramble, but Chloe backed him away and Luis used everything he had to pull me back.

She called me a dirty word and told Donnie they were leaving as he wiped off the spit with his sleeve. Then she turned to me. "Get out of here right now. And don't even think about coming back to work on that playground—I'll see you in court."

With that, they walked out the front door and we went out the back to get my car. I punched a tree on the way out and am pretty sure I broke my knuckle. It made writing pretty difficult for a while. Probably the maddest I have ever been.

Luis tried talking to me about it on the way home that night, but I wanted none of it. I took him home and then drove around for a while to cool down. When I got to Sara's later, she was already in bed, thankfully. I didn't want her to see me that angry.

I did recount all of the pills in Sara's cabinet before I went to bed. Let's just say it wasn't good.

Then I might have taken a few.

40

I was still fuming when I showed up to the coffee shop the next morning to meet Yeshua.

We sat down with our food and, after a few minutes of small talk, he asked, "Jack, what's wrong? You are not yourself this morning."

"Oh, nothing. Just that my life is falling apart." He squinted his eyes, wanting me to talk more. "You're *Jesus*, remember? Shouldn't you know what's going on? Or do you want to go ahead and give up the act now?"

He paused for a moment. "I love to hear things from your perspective—so I can know you and not just what's going on."

I huffed and decided to just spill it. Who else did I have to talk to? "I am just so very pissed off. The thought of Donnie Clark being at my house makes me…" I couldn't even finish the sentence because I was afraid I'd get emotional. "And I can't believe Chloe is going to divorce me. There's no hope for us getting back together, is there?"

"There is always hope."

"Well, it doesn't seem like it, if I know Chloe. I just hate it because it seems like some cruel joke—that the second I wake up from being an idiot and get my head on straight, I realize that it's a second too late to do anything about it. Irreparable damage. And I get to live with it for the rest of my life."

"Consequences are part of life, Jack. But you don't yet know if that is true for you and Chloe. There very well may be hope for your marriage—*if* you are willing to fight for it. You just have to decide how hard you want to fight."

"What else can I do?" I said, overwhelmed. "I'm willing to do anything to fight for it. But I don't know what to do—"

"You pursue her like your life depends on it. Repent over and over to her. Show her you are serious. Show her you care. Show her how hard you are willing to work."

"She won't talk to me—she won't even listen to me—so how do I do those things?"

"You are a writer—write her letters. Everyday if you have to. She will pretend to not care and not read them. But trust me, she will. At some point she will."

I sat back. "I hate myself."

"Hate what you've done, but not yourself. That goes nowhere good—"

"Man," I interrupted. "I don't know if I can take your pontificating today. Church, gospel…blah blah blah. Not when my life is crumbling to pieces."

He smiled and looked at me with tender eyes and started to say something, but then he stopped himself. "Of course we don't have to talk about any of that stuff today. That's part of what I want you to understand—that you get *me*. You get me on days that you just want to talk. Or on days that you don't want to talk, but just sit and be. I am always up for those times." We sat quietly for a few moments.

"So what do you want to do today?" he asked. "What do you feel up for? Anything?"

I thought for a bit. "Can we go and just sit at Mom's grave for a while?"

"Sure, Jack. Of course we can."

41

We get there and sit down on the small granite wall right beside Mom's grave. Maybe thirty minutes go by. Maybe an hour. I don't know. Silence is golden, though.

"I miss her so much," I finally say. "I wish she was here so badly. She was the best listener I've ever met."

"I know you do, Jack," his voice a little quivery, and I look over to see that his eyes are moist.

"Are you crying?" I ask. He doesn't answer. "Why are you crying?"

He doesn't say anything.

And I don't know why I say this, except out of desperate hope that it might be true. "I wish...you really were Jesus so you could just raise my mom from the dead."

"Jack," he says, wiping his face. "As much as I'd love to do that, I'm afraid I can't. Not exactly the way it works."

"Of course," I say. "I suppose this is where you give me the speech about heaven and how that's your plan to redeem all this mess, huh?"

"No," he answers. "This is not where that happens. Not the right time."

We sat there without talking for a bit longer.

It was nice to just sit there and think and not have to say anything.

"Oh yeah, I almost forgot," I said. "I'm getting more worried about Sara. Like I said the other night, she's using pills again and who knows what else. And she's wearing long sleeves a lot so I assume she is cutting again. I don't know what to do."

"Try to talk to her as much as you can, and try to get her to talk to you. I know it's hard with her—just do everything you can to let her know you want to help. And do everything you can to get her to go to this." He tells me the name of a recovery ministry at a local church.

"If you can get her to go there, she will find others who will care about her and hopefully she will let them help her."

"I'm really worried about her. I never was able to protect her. And I worry that even now I won't be able to do anything to help her. It's like there is this huge wall between us."

"Hey—don't blame yourself for not being able to protect her. That was not your job."

"I'm her big brother—how is that not my job?"

"I'm not saying you don't look out for her now—I'm saying that her past is not your responsibility. It was her dad's job to take care of her and he is the failure. Not you. You understand?"

He is poking me in the arm by this time, he's so insistent, but I just sit there and don't say a word. Staring into space.

"Jack—what happened to Sara is not your fault."

I don't flinch, even while he's pushing me.

Louder this time, he says, "Jack—what happened to Sara is not your fault." I feel my insides shaking, stirring. Another minute of silence goes by, and then he reaches up and puts his hand on my shoulder like a father would.

"Jack—I need you to hear this—what happened to Sara is not…"

I stop him mid-sentence by whirling around and knocking his arm off of my shoulder. "Listen," I say, quick and heavy. "Were *you* there when he was doing that stuff to her? Were *you* a part of all of her nightmares? Were *you* the only person in the world who could have done anything about it?" His face turned paper white and I don't think he even breathed. "Do *you* have to go through life wondering every single day why you couldn't have been just a little bit stronger, a little bit smarter—a little bit braver, so that you could have done something, anything, to save her from some of that pain? Do *you* see this canyon fixed between you and her every time you meet eyes with her because of what you shared together?" I stop for a moment to try to calm down, but I don't look away, not for a second.

"No? I didn't think so. So please, please—don't sit here and give me your little therapist spiel and think that I'm going to fall into your arms and cry like a baby. The bottom line is, I could have done something different. And I didn't."

I get up from the wall and pace around for a moment to try to keep my composure. But the eruption had just begun.

"In fact, *Jesus*, I should have asked you this all along: where the hell were you all of my life? Where were you when my dead-beat dad walked out on our family? Huh? Where were you when my uncle was abusing Sara and me—putting us through hell for a year? Where were you when Mom was hit by that drunk driver? *Where were you?* You weren't there! When I was the most hurt—the most alone and betrayed and could have really used a friend like you—you weren't there! Now look at us—Sara's been messed up her whole life and now my marriage is a train wreck, and you just waltz in here and you think you can preach a couple of sermons to me and be my friend and pretend that everything is going to be *fine*? That *you* are the solution to all of our problems? You're a quarter of a century too late for that."

We stand there in silence, both staring out over the cemetery. Finally, after a few frozen moments, he speaks:

"You're—you're right. I wasn't there. And I'm sorry."

I look at him, and notice for the first time that he has been crying. "What?" I say. "Where's the speech about how God is always there, whether you knew it or not—or God has a plan, all that sort of thing?"

"I wasn't there for you," he says, "but now I am." I stare at him, trying to figure him out. Jesus is apologizing to me? "I'm here. And I love you. Very much."

"So you're always gonna be here, in person, like this?" I ask. "To talk to me, to hang out, to call me out and to give me advice?"

He doesn't answer for the longest time, and then he just shakes his head. "You know it doesn't work like that, Jack. This is a special, limited time thing that can't last forever. But that doesn't mean that I'm leaving you—it means…it means you can have a relationship with me just like every other Christian, and one day you'll be with me forever—"

"Oh, cut the crap," I say. "Everyone I have ever loved has either left me, or has been taken away. I don't care if you are Jesus or a ballerina or a ticket-taker at the movies—but you're pretty much all I've got right now, so please don't leave me."

He gives me an anguished look, then shuffles his feet. "You're just like everyone else," I say. "Haven't I been abandoned enough?"

"Jack, come on—" he pleads. "That's not fair and you know it. You know this can't happen forever…let's talk about this."

I turn around and walk to my car, then stop for a moment and turn toward him before I get in. "Enjoy your life, *Jesus*." And I drive away, leaving him standing there in the cold with his hands stuck in his pockets.

42

I blackmailed Sara into going to Recovery that week. Told her that if she didn't start going with me every week that I was going to personally go up to her doctor's office and tell him about her abuse of the prescriptions, to at least cut off part of her supply. I wasn't sure it would work, but luckily it did.

We went to grab some dinner at Miyo's before. (Don't you just love Miyo's?) And she was having all kinds of fun with it. "So what is this gonna be like?" she asked. "Are these people going to try to exorcise me? I've seen that movie and I don't really want to go there."

I told her she was funny, and that I didn't really know what to expect honestly. Just that we had to do something and that a friend had recommended it to me.

We got there and walked in slowly, since we didn't know anyone. The thing met upstairs at this warehouse sort of building. A few people were at the front door to welcome us and introduce themselves. They didn't seem too creepy. Sara kept whispering things under her breath as we walked. "I bet that room is where they keep the really satanic people..." Then she growled at me like she was possessed.

We walked into the big room where the meeting was held and sat down beside each other on a couch. People were just milling around, talking, and a few more people came up and said hello to us. There were maybe forty people there, of all ages and backgrounds it seemed.

After a few minutes went by, the main leader went up to the podium and motioned for everyone to sit down, and said that we were starting. He was a bigger guy in his thirties with a thick beard, and he seemed cool enough. "My name is Allen," he said. "Welcome to Recovery, everyone—we have a few new people tonight, so I just want to say a special welcome to you." He looked at Sara and me, along with a few others. "This is a safe place for you. We have a nice little family here and we are all about finding healing and freedom from the things in our lives that seem unbeatable. We believe that hope and healing is found in Jesus and his work in our lives, and we will talk more about that later." With that, he prayed and some guy with a guitar stood up to play a few worship songs. Sara just kept looking at me and widening her eyes, as if to ask me why I'd brought her to this crazy house.

The guy finished and Allen went back up to the podium to teach the lesson. He picked up his Bible and read some verses about how Jesus says he is the truth, and that the truth will set you free. Something like that. He went on in the lesson to talk about what he called the battle between truth and feelings. All of this Jesus stuff—I had no idea what I believed about all this. I was just glad that Sara was hearing it. And I hoped she was listening.

He went on a bit more and talked about how Jesus can set us free from being slaves to lies and feelings. That we could have peace in him because he never changes and never leaves us. Some more stuff like that. Then he prayed, and said we were going to break up into male and female groups. Sara gave me an "are you kidding me?" look. I just winked at her at walked out of the room with the rest of the guys.

On my way to the guys' meeting room, I saw Luis. He must have slipped in late and sat in the floor behind us.

"Hey buddy!" I said, walking up to him. "I didn't know you were going to be here."

"*Hola!*" he said, perking up when he recognized who I was. "Yes, I be here. This is my family. Glad you made it, brother!"

"Hey, sorry about the other night—" I said.

"No," he said, drawing it out. "No sorry. No reason."

We walked together to the classroom and I sat down beside him. After everyone came in, Allen stepped over and closed the door, then sat down in the circle. He looked over at me and asked my name. I told him and then he explained that when they have a new person, they all go around and introduce themselves and tell a little about why they are there.

They started up—I don't really remember most of them, but I remember being surprised at some of their reasons for being there. It was way more than just drug and alcohol addiction. Some were abused, dealing with depression, etc.

Eventually, we got to a guy named Edmond. He introduced himself to me with a very proper sounding voice. "And we are glad to have you Jack." He was a large African American man, probably in his fifties, dressed very nicely. "The reason I am here is that I was an alcoholic for years and years, and then I was addicted to cocaine for several years..." he paused, like he was preparing for good news. "Although...this week I picked up my one year chip," he got out his keychain and held up an NA key ring. I smiled at him while the rest of the group clapped and cheered.

"And..." he continued, "I struggle with depression at times. That's me—but I don't want to take up too much time." He elbowed the guy sitting beside him.

The next guy was a young white guy who I had seen come in earlier. He was disabled and pushed along a silver walker with red handles. He looked about as innocent as could be and I couldn't imagine why he would be here.

"My name is Frank," he said, straightening in his chair, his voice much deeper than I expected. "And I'm here, I guess, because of drugs. Mostly prescription stuff, but other stuff too." I didn't quite know what to think about Frank, but he seemed like a cool guy I'd like to hang out with.

"Hola," Luis said. He was up next. "My name is Luis, though you already know me, hehe." He pointed at me and laughed. "And I am alcoholic. Used to drink rubbing alcohol, but now it's just King Cobras, so that's good!" His joke didn't quite take with the group.

He winked at me and smiled, "Good to have you here, buddy."

I've never used the adjective "adorable" to describe a man before, and I hesitate to use it now because you might think less of me, but I might have to use it for Luis. He is awesome.

A few more went, and then the next guy I remember was an older African American man, skinny and tall with grey puffs of hair. "My name Willie." He stopped and smacked his lips, obviously missing some teeth from the way he talked. "Willie Smith," (it came out "Smif") "Junior. I'm here because I been addicted to drugs for most of my life. I'm in NA now, and I come here too because the more meetings I can go to, the better." His voice was scruffy, and I thought I had a vague memory of him asking me for money once in Five Points.

Are you the type who would give money, or the type who doesn't, thinking they'll just spend it on drugs? I wonder.

"We're glad to have you, Jack." He put his hands on his knees, then stood up and walked across the room. I got nervous, not knowing what he was going to do. He came right in front of me. "Gimme a hug." I looked around the room and everyone was smiling, oozing with awkwardness.

"Willie, I don't know if Jack is ready for a hug yet—" Allen interjected. I was weirded out something serious, but decided to not make the situation any worse. "No, it's okay." I stood up and gave Willie a very awkward one-armed hug. Then he turned around and went back to his chair. Everyone was still smiling except him— he was oblivious.

I don't really remember many of the others. Certain people just stick out to you, you know?

The last person to go was an older white man named Ron. He had kind eyes that said they'd been through a lot, and there was something comforting about his voice. Deep and raspy. "Hey Jack," he introduced himself. "My name is Ron. To give you the short version, I was a professional counselor for many years when I was younger. Then I got over my head into the party scene, and I got hooked on every drug you can imagine. I lost everything—my house, my money, my cars—and the worst part was losing a lot of my friends to addiction. It is an absolute miracle I'm still alive, and I'm doing much better, but I still struggle with drugs occasionally. But I've been clean for a few months as well."

I nodded my head to him and said, "Thanks Ron, nice to meet you."

"Likewise."

"Jack, would you like to share a little bit about why you are here?" Allen asked, all eyes on me.

"Sure," I said, clearing my throat. "My name is Jack, obviously. You already know that. Honestly, there is nothing going on with me, I am just here to support my sister, Sara. She really struggles with, well, a lot of stuff. She's tried to commit suicide before and I am getting more worried about her these days, so I made her come with me here. So yeah—that's why I'm here—I don't have any *serious* issues like you guys…"

Oops. I didn't mean for it to come out like that. Like many other times, my mouth just seems to have a foot-shaped hole in it. I tried to find a way to make it sound better, but Frank beat me to the punch.

"You don't have to be a self-righteous prick about it," he said, rolling his eyes.

"Hey—" Allen interjected, glaring at Frank.

"No, it's okay," I responded. "I'm sorry—that didn't come out right. Didn't mean it like that."

Edmond told me it was okay and came to my rescue by making a joke about everyone loving Frank because he just says what he thinks.

Afterward, Allen approached me when I was standing off to myself. He said a few pleasantries, it was nice to have me, etc. Then he got a serious look on his face. "You are Jack Bennett, from *The State*, aren't you?"

Suddenly I got a little worried. "Yes, I am. I didn't know you would recognize me."

"Just curious…is there another reason why you are here?" I thought for a second about what he was implying.

"Oh, no—no. I get it now. No—I promise I am here for Sara and no other reason. I guess that does look fishy considering the piece I wrote a while back."

"Yeah, well, I'm still glad you are here. I hope it will be good for you in some way at least. I did need to make sure there were no ulterior motives in coming here, since this is a confidential environment and all. You understand?"

"Absolutely."

He asked me if I'd like to get together sometime, and I said sure. I could use all the friends I could get, I figured.

After he left, Frank came by and stopped. "Hey man, we cool?"

I smiled at him. "Yeah man, we're cool. Sorry, I didn't mean it like that. I appreciate your candor."

"There ain't no sense in bullshittin', as far as I'm concerned," he said, smiling.

"You're right," I said. "I think we could get along well."

"Well, hey, man," he said. "I can read people, okay?" He looked at me like I should know what he was saying. I didn't follow, so he kept going.

"I can tell you got more going on than you're letting on." He let that sink in for a minute. "So if you want to talk about any of it, I'm game."

I didn't really know how to respond to that. It's not like I could call his bluff. "Okay."

The girls were finishing up right about then, so Sara and I said goodbye and walked out to the car.

"So how was it? What happened?" I asked.

"You'll never believe it Jack—" she said, like she was about to tell me she won the lottery. "I was sitting there in the room while they were talking about how the truth will set you free, and all of a sudden this light shone from above us," she waved her hands, "right onto me, and there were angels coming down from this ladder, and they grabbed me and poured water all over me, and they said, 'Sara, you are free! You were dirty, but now you've been made clean!'"

I rolled my eyes. "So did you listen to anything at all, or did you just spend the entire time coming up with that ridiculous story?"

"Mostly just came up with the story." She smiled again and I didn't smile back. I exhaled and started up the engine to go home.

We didn't get far, however, because Willie walked in front of our headlights and waved his arms to get my attention. I rolled the window down as he walked over.

"What's up, Willie? You need something?"

"What way y'all headin?" he asked. I told him, and then he asked if we could maybe take him home. I introduced him to Sara and he immediately turned on the charm.

"My pleasure to meet you, Sara," he said. "My name Willie."

We drove through Five Points on the way to his apartment, and he said something that took me off guard. "Hey, while I'm thinking straight, Jack—if I ever ask you to take me to Five Points, don't do it."

"Okay…" I answered.

In the rearview mirror I saw him scratch his chin like he was thinking real hard, and then he said, "You know what I always say…"

"What?"

"You know what I always say…" he repeated, in the exact same voice.

"Um, no, I don't. What do you always say?"

"If you hang around a barbershop long enough, you gon' end up gettin a haircut."

Sara and I both laughed at that, and he chimed in, happy to get the response he wanted.

"It's true," he said, still smiling.

"Yeah it is, Willie. That's a good way to put it."

43

What are the things that you think, but you would never tell anyone or say out loud?

I know that's getting kind of personal. And we're not quite friends yet. But I've been thinking about that. And by the way, I hope you can trust me when we get to talk. Especially since I've told you all this stuff about myself.

Do you want to hear one thing that I think a lot that I've never said out loud? I guess I'll tell you, seeing that you can't really answer me yet. There are cons to this really long letter deal after all. Maybe I should have just walked up to you and started talking. But that probably would have been even weirder. And I needed to get all this out.

Okay, so sometimes, I'll see people, let's say I'm at a restaurant, and I see a group of friends laughing and having drinks, just acting like they are having a blast, and I'll think to myself, I bet if I was with them I would be happy. Or I'll be driving down my neighborhood road and I'll see a family outside playing in the front yard, in front of their picture perfect house, and I'll think, I bet if I had that I'd be happy.

Now here's the tricky part. I do have that. Or at least, I had that. Dream house. Dream family. That's not what I mean. What I mean, when I have those thoughts, is, I bet if I had *that* family and *that* house I would be happy—like if somehow I switched lives with them I would be happy, because they are clearly happy. I mean, look at them, playing with their dog in the front yard. It's a golden retriever for crying out loud. They don't have problems like I have. Their life is perfect and they have to pinch themselves every morning they are so happy.

Or even worse—this is embarrassing because of how much I hate advertising—I'll see a billboard of some resort in the mountains or something, or a Corona commercial, and I'll think the same thing. If I went there or if I lived there I'd be happy. It'd be impossible not to be, right?

I'm embarrassed to admit all of that. I guess that's why I've never said it to anyone before. It all just seems incredibly inane—as if I've ever met anyone whose life was perfect. But the sad thing is that during those moments, I really believe it. I mean, believe it like, *the earth is round* believe it.

So Friday night Sara and I were finishing up dinner at the apartment, and there's a knock on the door. I opened the door and stepped outside on the porch, pulling the door closed behind me.

"Hey," Yeshua says, turning his gaze downward.

"Hey," I respond and then stand there looking at my toes. I finally spoke up to break the ensuing silence.

"I'm sorry about the other day."

"It's okay, Jack. I'm sorry, too."

I tilted my head and thumbed my belt loop, trying to figure out what was going on and what I thought about all of this. Finally, I said, "What's this all about? Really?"

He shrugged his shoulders and asked me what I meant.

I could tell he wasn't going to answer me, and since I didn't know what else to say, after an awkward minute or so I exhaled and said, "Want to come in?"

"Sure," he said. "That sounds great. We've got some time yet." I nodded my head, unsure of what to say.

He looked up with a grin. "You guys play poker?"

"You gamble? I'm not really the type to play for Skittles."

"How about a $10 buy-in? Winner takes all."

We pitched the idea to Sara, and she was in.

"All right, no cheating now, you too," Yeshua said as he dealt the first hand. "I don't want to see any shenanigans."

The three ten dollar bills were stacked in the middle of the table, and Sara was giddy. "I feel like I'm at one of those tournaments on ESPN," she said. "Except I need some sunglasses or something. Hold on." She ran to get her sunglasses from her room.

"You are ridiculous…" I said when she got back.

"I gotta do anything I can to improve my poker face!"

"True. You've never been very good at hiding stuff."

I won the first hand with two pair, but the bets were low. I got up to get out the chips and salsa out, and I grabbed a Duck-Rabbit Milk Stout for each of us. Have you ever had DR? *So good.*

We played for an hour or so, each going down and up a bit, and then Sara gave me the sign (three scratches on her left cheek). The plan was that when she was tired of playing, she would very confidently go all in on a crappy hand and I would go in with her, and I would get all of her donated chips to bully Yeshua with until I finished him off. It was a trick I learned back in college when I didn't have the attention span for poker, so I'd work the deal out with a friend and then split the pot with him. I got a little nervous this time because my hand was awful, but our plan worked. Yeshua dropped out before we even went all in.

"You win," Sara said, laying down her cards.

We kept playing for a while longer, and I unfortunately lost a few big hands until we were about even. Somehow Yeshua seemed to instantly get much better at poker. I mean, if the guy was really Jesus, wouldn't he know what my cards were? Was Jesus a mind reader? Or omniscient or whatever?

Whoever he was, he was a poker shark. I was down to three chips within four hands, and then I shortly lost those. He beat me mercilessly. And I was, I'm proud to admit, a grown-up about it. Even if he did use divine telepathy to win. And then he took the money and gave it to Sara, calling her the "real winner" because of her good attitude. I told both of them I was going to vomit.

Before he left that night, he asked if he could cook Thanksgiving dinner for us the next week.

I don't know why, but we said yes.

Yeshua, Jesus, whatever—he's all we had.

44

I've only told you a little bit about my favorite music. You need to know that to really know someone, you know? I hope we can share songs one day. There's really not much better than when someone loves the same music as much as you do.

I hope this is not like one of those times where you love a song or a band, and you play it for one of your friends and they just give you a blank stare and hate it. That's awful.

I like a lot of different stuff, and I know I've already told you some. What haven't I told you about? Well, there's Frightened Rabbit—their song "The Loneliness and the Scream" is so much fun. I love Bon Iver and James Vincent McMorrow. Probably two of my all-time favorites, so if you know either of them then you know my taste in music pretty well. Ray LaMontagne. Ryan Adams. William Fitzsimmons. I could listen to him all day. Explosions in the Sky. I am crushing instrumental stuff these days.

Speaking of Explosions in the Sky—I just thought of something. Have you ever watched *Friday Night Lights*? The TV show, not the movie. It is *incredible*. The writers do such a good job of making you care about the characters, and Coach Taylor is one of my favorite characters ever. I would follow that man into the open mouth of a lion.

Clear eyes...full hearts...can't lose.

Okay, back to music. Older stuff would include Taking Back Sunday and The Appleseed Cast. A very different band I like is called Listener. Look up the music video of the song "Wooden

Heart" sometime and see if it doesn't punch you in the chest. I love Mat Kearney, and I love Bob Dylan. If you don't love Bob Dylan, then you're just un-American.

Of course I love old school country like Garth Brooks. And Johnny Cash. Have you ever heard his cover of the song "Hurt"? Man, it will kill you.

A local band that I really like is called Toro y Moi. You might have heard them since they are getting bigger these days. Also, Valleymaker. Austin Crane, the lead singer, used to work at Immac so you've probably seen him. He is such a cool guy. They recently released an album that is a really interesting narrative of Old Testament stories, and although that is a little odd for my taste, it is one of the most beautiful albums I've ever heard. I've got it on vinyl and it's amazing. On the more upbeat side, The Glitch Mob…they are so good and fun to listen to. If you listen to "Drive It Like You Stole It" and don't smile and tap your foot there is something wrong with you.

I told you I had an eclectic interest in music. It would be cool if we already share some favorites.

So that Saturday night, I went to bed early with a bit of an upset stomach. Sometimes my love for hot sauce gets the best of me.

Anyway, I got up around midnight to go to the bathroom. I was on the way back to my room, and I thought I heard Sara crying. I could barely see her around the corner in the living room, but it was dark enough in the back that she couldn't see me.

She wasn't crying hard, just sniffling a little, and she wiped a few tears away. I thought about going in there to try to talk to her, but I decided to wait. She was reading something, but I couldn't tell what it was.

After a few minutes, I decided to check on her.

"Sara? Are you okay?"

I went and sat down beside her on the couch. She just sat there for a minute trying to dry up, and then told me that she was fine. "Yeah, it seems like it," I said, trying to lighten the mood. "You can tell me what's wrong, you know. I'm cool." She didn't say anything, but she did lean her head over on my shoulder, and I put my arm around her and squeezed her. That was probably one of my favorite moments ever with her.

After a few minutes I asked her what she was reading and she said it was a letter. She didn't want to, but after a few minutes of me bugging her about it because I thought it was someone being mean to her, she handed it to me and said, "Here, read it," while wiping her nose with her sleeve. It was a hand-written letter on yellow-lined paper—no signature at the bottom—filled with encouraging words for her. Words that I could never say to Sara, words like "you're loved" and "you're beautiful" and "you are worth so much more than you think."

At the bottom of the letter was a verse from the Bible.

"The Lord your God is with you, he is mighty to save. He will take great delight in you, he will quiet you with his love, he will rejoice over you with singing." Zephaniah 3.17

"Do you know who wrote it?"

"No," she said.

I thought maybe it was Yeshua, trying to sprinkle his magic fairy Jesus dust on her. The man just doesn't stop.

"Is it the first?"

"No," she said, sniffling. "They started coming about a year ago. I don't know why I still cry—it's just the same old bullshit."

So it wasn't him—he only met Sara a few weeks before. I sat there with my arm around her for a while longer, her head still resting on my shoulder. After a few minutes, she remembered her self-imposed rule to always be tough and hard, so she got up and said she was going to bed. I stood next to her, kissed her on the forehead and told her I loved her. She didn't respond, just curled the left side of her mouth up and walked away to her bedroom, still holding the letter.

45

The next morning I met Yeshua, usual time, usual place. After breakfast, we strolled around downtown for a while and ended up in Finlay Park. We sat down on one of the steps in the amphitheater and watched all the people spread through the park. People running. Walking dogs. College students throwing frisbees. Families having picnics.

"This really makes me miss my family."

"I know," he said. "I'm sure it does."

"I wrote her a letter this week," I said. "And then I got the divorce papers later that day."

I had also burned a copy of a song that I heard called "Rivers and Roads" by The Head and The Heart and sent it to her. It seemed appropriate because I knew she would love it, and it talked about missing someone like hell and being willing to cross rivers and roads to reach them. But I figured she probably trashed it.

"Hang in there, Jack. Keep going—keep pursuing her. Maybe you can do a little more now that she's had some space. Try to go over there and talk to her. Go get the kids if she will let you. Send her flowers. Do whatever you can."

I sat there, not saying anything—thinking about how all my efforts were probably destined to fail.

"One letter isn't going to go very far in the face of all that pain. You may have to lay down in front of her car to show her you are serious, because right now she still doesn't believe you."

"I know," I said, still dejected.

"But at what point in this process do I just give up and go back to Jordan before she's gone too?"

Before I even knew it he had reached up and slapped me across the back of the head.

And I mean slapped. Hard.

"Ouch!" I screamed. "Are you kidding me? You're gonna slap me?"

"You needed it for saying something stupid like that. It's time for you to grow up and be a man instead of just being a boy who can shave."

This coming from the guy who thinks he's Jesus, I thought. "All right, let's get on with our Sunday School lesson for the morning. I'm sure you've got some more preaching to do. There, you can use that rail as your podium, and I'll sit here like a good little parishioner."

He let out a quiet, disgusted kind of laugh and shook his head. "Nah," he said. "No preaching today. I'm not in the mood." He shuffled his feet in the gravel below the step.

I looked around the park for a minute, then back at him. "Fine with me," I said. "By the way, I figured out another reason why I don't buy all of your sin, cross, gospel spiel."

"Yeah? What's that," he said, not looking at me. Like he was half there and half somewhere else.

"All of your talk about how broken and wicked and selfish I am—how much of a sinner and all, I kind of get that in a way. I know I'm messed up. But honestly from there, the way you say that there's nothing I can do about it and all, how Jesus has to do it because he's perfect and I'm just a screw up—it makes me feel like God is just like my dad was. He never cared about anything I did, never paid me any attention. Nothing I did could ever measure up, nothing could make him proud. And it sounds like God is the exact same way—I'm just a screw up who he just gets mad at, and Jesus is like the perfect older brother who heroically somehow pays for my mistakes and then God decides to tolerate me again and is not pissed at me anymore…hooray!"

He gave me a look, then exhaled and sat there. It seemed like he really just wanted to get up and walk off. "Jack," he said after a few minutes, then paused. "I get it. I know you're pissed. And you are confused. You had a terrible earthly father, and fathers are supposed to be the examples of God for their kids. So you project your picture of your father onto God, and that gets all kinds of messy." He stopped for a minute. "Do you remember much about your father, or is it all impressions?"

I thought for a moment, then told him not much specifically, other than that he was pissed all the time, yelled a lot, and seemed to not notice my presence. I told him about dropping the coffee pot the day he left, and that for years I thought he really left because I dropped the coffee pot.

He bit his lip and stared into space for a while before responding. When he finally did, he said, "You remember playing Little League baseball, Jack?" I was confused, but told him yes and he went on. "I bet when you played, especially when you did something good like make a great play in the field or hit a homerun, you would look around the stands and wish that your dad was there, wouldn't you? That he was there to see you perform and pat you on the back and tell you he's proud of you?"

I didn't answer.

"Human nature is performance-based to the core, Jack. You want to earn your value and standing before God—to measure up and prove your worth. You may think you want God to be that kind of father—the kind that pushes you and only stands up and claps for you when you hit a homerun, when you succeed or perform well. But that's not the kind of father you really want, or need for that matter. Be honest with yourself—is that really what you want? If your value comes from measuring up or hitting a homerun, what happens to your value when you strike out?

"God is not some cold, emotionless father that pays no attention to you. He is a loving, affectionate, gracious father. Despite your rebelling against him and choosing a different father, he chases you down, pursues you—so you can be reconciled to him. So you can be adopted back into his family. He is the kind of father that takes you in his arms, even when you strike out to lose the game. He's the kind of father that covers you with his grace when you drop the proverbial coffee pot. He's the kind of father that runs down the street to meet his prodigal son who just completely betrayed him and chose a different family.

"And you are right," he said. "The first message of the cross is that you are more wicked than you will ever realize—that your sin necessitated such a gruesome, bloody death to atone for your rebellion. Nothing pretty or heart-warming about that…the gospel damns before it sets you free. But it cannot stop there, Jack—it can't stop there because that's not the whole gospel. The second message of the cross is simultaneously that you are more loved than you could ever dream, that God himself was willing—was glad—to become human and die for you."

"You mean *you* were willing to become human and die for me, right?" I interjected.

"Right," he said dismissively. "Here is the bottom line Jack. God did not bail on you or your family—you bailed on him and his family, said 'screw you' and left. For no reason other than that he loves you desperately, he went to great lengths to invite you back into his family. It might feel more complicated than that to you, but it's not. It's that simple. The gospel doesn't take away your worth, it gives you your worth. It turns runaway traitors into sons and daughters of the king—into children whose value comes only from the father's love, not from their performance! God does not just tolerate sinners who are adopted through Jesus—he radiates affection and approval over them, and their betrayal will never be remembered by him.

"The father loves you and wants you back," he said, and it felt for the first time that he wasn't just giving me a spiel or a tract —he actually felt it deep within him.

"No matter where you are or what you've done, he wants you back. He has gone to great lengths to get you back at his table. All of the father issues from all of the broken families in the world —including yours—can be healed by that reality. What you always wanted from your father is yours a hundred times over in the gospel, Jack—the unbridled affection and delight of God, not predicated on your performance."

I thought about saying something really awful, but I refrained. He nervously patted his knees as if he would be happy to move on. Finally, I decided to take it easy on him and said, "What a liar…"

He looked at me, confused.

"You said you weren't gonna preach today."

He laughed and said that I made him—that I twisted his arm and I said I did no such thing. Then he stood up and asked me if I wanted to go to The Whig to get a burger and talk about less serious stuff. I said yes and was thankful to leave.

46

It's funny to sit here and write this to you, watching you and you have no idea. It's still crazy to have a face for you. Whatever you're working on must be a *beast*. I can't believe I've gotten this far in one sitting.

I hope when we get to meet that you won't hide things from me. You won't, will you? Because, let's be honest—all of us are hiding. Hiding behind an infinite amount of masks that we don and exchange with the skill of Houdini. As honest as I've been with you so far—as far out into the light as I've come—I'm still hiding. Things are worse than I let on. This is no news. We are all far more broken than we let on. I've learned that lately, that's for sure. But, have you ever stopped to wonder what it means that we are hiding? That we are so afraid to be real with one another that we will go to any length to keep that from happening?

The more I think about it, it has to come down to acceptance. Is that not what we all want? The frantic searching that you feel, wanting others to approve you? All you have to do is watch a group of middle school kids for a while to see this. And I don't know about you, but this is pretty much at the core of everything I do. I try to manage my impression to literally everyone I meet, thus precluding the possibility of anyone at all really knowing me. Because I'm always lying to them, always putting on these acts. It's not only counter-productive—it's exhausting.

But slowly, very slowly, something is happening inside of me. All of the different Jack's are slowly becoming one Jack. Does that sound pretentious to speak of myself in the third person? I don't mean it to. What I mean is, there used to be a Work Jack, a Home Jack, an Out With The Boys Jack, a Nice To Meet You I Hope You Think I'm Awesome Jack, and so on. You understand. The masks. Have you ever been fighting with your spouse or friend or someone on the way to somewhere, mad as anything, and then when you get out of the car at so-and-so's place, you undergo an instant conversion to Nice and Happy you? I bet you have.

I still have a long way to go, but they are slowly starting to come off, to meld into one Jack that is just me, plain and simple. Wherever I'm at and whoever I'm with.

I hope the trend continues, because it is some kind of freeing.

Monday evening after work I went to the parking lot of Gold's Gym and parked beside Chloe's Audi. Every Monday, Wednesday, and Friday she got a babysitter for a few hours so she could go to the gym. I parked beside her and waited.

I had been there for twenty-five minutes or so when she walked out. Ponytail, spandex pants and her usual workout tank top. So gorgeous.

I got out of my car and stood beside hers. When she got close enough to see me she paused and rolled her head back. "Jack —what are you doing here?"

"I came to talk. What else do you expect when you won't answer my phone calls or the door when I come to my own house?"

"It's not your house anymore. Half of it isn't, at least." I took a deep breath.

"Chloe, we are not getting a divorce. I won't sign those papers. I already told you. I want to fix things."

"Fix things?" she bowed up. "Fix things? Did you bring a hammer and a wrench? It's not that simple, Jack. You are not smooth-talking yourself out of this one."

"Chloe, come on—I'm not trying to smooth-talk anyone. I promise you, I really am different now. I am so sorry. I'm not giving up on us, on our family."

"You gave up a long time ago, Jack." She was getting every ounce of sting possible in.

"Did you read my letter?"

"Nope." I didn't know if she really had or not, but she sure wasn't going to let me know she did. I bent down and put my head in my right hand. I asked her if she had listened to the song and she fired another nope.

"Are you still seeing Donnie?"

"Yes—no. I'm still officially married, so I wouldn't do anything yet. Unlike some people."

"Did you just go out and find him to make me angry?"

"No, Jack. I just connected with him on Facebook one day and told him what was going on. He offered to take me out a few times to get some time away. Because he is a gentleman."

A few words ran through my mind for what Donnie was, and none of them were gentleman. But I held my tongue. "After all these years of marriage, and all we have been through together…" I paused to think. "You are seriously not going to even consider reconciling with me, giving me a second chance? I am your husband."

"And I was your wife. After all these years of marriage and all we've been through—"

I was running out of ideas. "Chloe, if you are just trying to punish me before you give me a second chance, will you please stop? I hate myself enough for the both of us, I assure you."

"I'm not trying to punish you. I wouldn't willingly hurt *you*. Even after everything you have done."

I bent down and rubbed my eyes again.

"What can I do to prove to you that I am different? That I really am serious?"

"It doesn't matter if you can prove it to me or not. You being serious isn't all there is to this equation. Now will you please move?" I was standing in front of her door. "I have to get home to take care of my kids."

"*Our* kids. *Our kids.* And you can't just keep me from seeing them. They are my kids too and I miss them terribly."

"You can see them when the judge works out custody times."

I huffed and crossed my arms over my chest. "Come on, Chloe. Please stop this."

"Okay," she finally acquiesced. "You can pick up the kids Saturday. I have a party to go to anyway."

"Please tell me it's not with Donnie."

"I'll tell you it's none of your business," she said. "Now move, please." I stepped out of the way and she got in her car.

She backed out and drove away without looking at me again.

47

My phone rang when I was leaving Gold's Gym. I didn't recognize the number but picked up anyway for some reason. I never do that.

"Hello?"

"*Hola amigo*! How you been?"

"Fine," I said, irritated. "How are you?"

"Fine, fine. Something wrong? You don't sound good."

"No, I'm okay. Just been a long day. Thanks for asking though."

He went on to ask me what I was doing that night. I said nothing. Don't you hate when this happens—when someone first finds out you have nothing to do, then asks you to do something? I do. I feel like I've been tricked, and like I can't lie and say I have something else going on anymore. I have to either just be mean and say I don't want to or make up an excuse. Which, I'm a pretty skilled excuse maker, but still. I hate that.

He asked me to go to some church thing with him—I couldn't really understand what he was saying. Something about a family meeting or something, and I didn't know what that was. I resisted, told him I was tired and needed some rest. He persisted. "Come on buddy, should be fun. If you don't enjoy it I will give you your money back…"

Finally, he pulled the "that's fine if you don't want to hang out with me" card, after offering to buy me dinner.

And I gave in. He must have had some kind of magic Mexican persuasive powers.

I went and picked him up and we ended up at the meeting late. Evidently he didn't know this since he offered me dinner, but it was a potluck. We were the slackers who walked in after everyone else had fixed their plates and sat down. And we didn't bring anything. Of course.

Things got worse. After we made our plates and sat down at a round table with a group of people, they started introducing themselves to me. They knew Luis already, of course. Then one of them asked me how long I'd been a member, and I almost choked on my tea. "Not long," I said, and tried not to say anything after that.

I got up to find Allen. Luckily I caught him while he was going for a refill. "Hey Allen—" I said, red-faced. "Somehow Luis talked me into coming here and I had no idea it was a member's meeting. I'm so embarrassed. I'm going to leave, will you find him a ride home?"

"Jack," he reached out and shook my hand, smiling. "Sorry about that—but would you please stay? Good food. Nice people. And I promise no one will know that you are not a member—"

"What are y'all gonna do, pull out snakes or something? I didn't bring my anti-venom…"

He roared at that. "No, not exactly. But stay, really. I'd love for you too. I will introduce you to my wife and some of the guys from Recovery are here and they would love to see you." I was quite unhappy about it, but eventually I surrendered and went back to my seat.

I whispered to Luis, "You didn't tell me this was a member's meeting—I'm not supposed to be here."

He looked at me and furrowed his brow like it was the most outlandish thought ever to occur to man. "No…" he drew it out, "nonsense. This is my family and you are part of my family too, buddy. You with me—you more than welcome." He smiled and put his hand on my shoulder. "Trust me."

How could you not love this guy?

Just a minute later some guy, another one of the pastors, went to the front and told everyone to grab their chairs and bring them up to the front because we were about to start. Allen and his wife found Luis and me during the mass exodus of a few hundred folding chairs and set up theirs beside us. The guy came back up, welcomed everyone and then went over some announcements. His name was Adam—a tall, skinny guy with a baseball cap and t-shirt and jeans on. Didn't exactly fit my mental image of a pastor.

He then proceeded to pull out his Bible and read some verse...all I remember is the word "repent" being in there somewhere. He said he was going to talk about repentance and asked us why we thought the word repent had a bad rap in our culture.

This guy with tattoos all over him stood up and yelled, "Because that guy in Five Points with the bullhorn always yells about repenting, and I don't like that guy." Everyone laughed and I'll admit, I did too.

The pastor guy went on to talk about repentance for a few minutes, basically saying that the opportunity to repent was a gift from God and not some lightning bolt threat from self-righteous religious people. He said that God was not some impersonal police officer writing us a ticket and wanting us to behave better like the bullhorn guy, but a loving father inviting us back into his family... blah blah blah. I get this all the time from Yeshua, I thought.

My mind wandered and I started thinking about Chloe. How I'd gotten so frustrated with her earlier because she wouldn't just take me back. And how angry I was that she was spending time with Donnie—at least she said they weren't serious. And then it hit me for the first time: not only did she not have to take me back, but for all practical purposes she shouldn't.

Why would she? Does someone deserve a second chance after they've done something that wrong? For some reason, I felt like I did. I have a pretty high estimate of myself, huh?

But if the shoe was on the other foot? No. You don't just get over a wound that deep.

Soon after in his talk, he switched gears and started talking about how somewhere along the line, Christians started believing that after they met Jesus they didn't have to repent anymore, that they were now in the "good" camp. Then he said, "I'll tell you where that gets you," and held up something in his hand. I squinted to see what it was.

He was holding up a copy of the Sunday paper with my column on the front page. I started to panic a bit, but Allen turned to whisper to me before I really had time to think, "Don't panic. I had no idea. No one knows you." I began to sweat a little, but nodded to him and remained outwardly calm at least.

"Did any of you read this article?" A good many people raised their hands, knowing what he was talking about. He went on to talk about how he hated that so many people in our country had that very impression of Christianity—all hypocrites and judgmental prudes—and said that the reason was that so many Christians had forgotten that they are called to a continual lifestyle of repentance. Not just a one time deal, but daily taking responsibility for their sin and turning from it. And not just the outward things, but pride, self-righteousness, greed, lack of compassion, etc. He went on to say that if Christians in our country took daily repentance seriously, that people would have a much better picture of Jesus and columns like mine wouldn't be written.

Then, I was really surprised, because he said they weren't going to just talk about repentance—they were going to practice it. He said that they were ending with communion and worship, but that first everyone needed to repent of anything they needed to. He told them to grab someone to confess to, and that if they'd sinned against someone, to grab that person or call them on the phone before they joined in worship. My eyes were glued open, thinking this was about to be fantastically awkward.

And it was. Oh, it was glorious. People sat there for a second like someone had just told them to jump off a bridge. They looked down at their feet, twiddled their thumbs, prayed. Or pretended to pray. I was eating it up.

Then, the silence broke with the lone squeal of a metal chair pushing against the floor.

A young girl stood up from her chair, tears in her eyes, and went to grab one of her friends.

That screech was the most humble sound I've ever heard.

And then, another. Then one more. And another. I guess the humility was contagious. Soon there were dozens of people up and about, talking with others or on their phones. Some guy with a guitar got on stage and started playing quietly.

I have to admit this, as much as I don't want to. It was one of the most beautiful things I've ever experienced.

Why is it that there is just something so moving about a heartfelt apology? When someone stops being prideful and owns their crap and really seems to be genuine about it—not the ones that just want something out of the deal. I don't know why this is true, but it is. That scene in the movies always gets me—the big re-conciliation scene.

I was handling this all pretty well that night, until I saw this happen: a husband grabbed his wife and took her over to the side to talk. I watched them from the corner of my eye, and for a minute it looked like things were getting heated. Very expressive hands were flying about. Then, the husband said something, and the wife exhaled a sob, then her eyes glistened and she put her arms around his neck. He wrapped his arms around her and picked her up off the floor he hugged her so tight.

Suddenly I felt an urge to get out of there.

48

That week Recovery was on Wednesday, since Thanksgiving was on Thursday. Sara agreed to go again, so we went to dinner at Hunter-Gatherer beforehand, and I tried to talk to her as much as she would let me. Which wasn't much.

"So sis, how are you doing this week? And don't lie to me, because I'm counting your pills."

"If you know then I don't have to tell you, I guess."

I frowned at her. "Come on Sara—I really wish you would talk to me about real stuff."

"Sure! What do you want to talk about?" she said.

"I want to talk about you. And for you not to mock me."

"That's your fault, Jack. You're just so perfectly mock-able."

I asked her if she was still seeing that guy, Aaron. "Yep. Far as I know," she said. I asked her if he treated her well and she said as well as can be expected.

"What does that mean?" I asked.

She rolled her eyes and muttered under her breath, "Not very well."

"Sara—"

"I'm just messing with you, Jack—he treats me fine. Maybe you'll meet him someday soon. But probably not." She gave me a fake smile.

We finished up dinner and headed to Recovery without me telling her what I really wanted to tell her. What I wanted to tell her every time I saw her. That I was sorry for being a part of her nightmare stories—and that I wasn't able to protect her. That I was sorry we couldn't really be close because of those things.

On the way to Recovery I did work up the courage to tell her the other thing that I always wanted to tell her, over and over again, to try to convince her that it was true.

"Sara, you know that Mom's death wasn't your fault, right? I know I've told you that a hundred times before, but I just want you to know it and believe it, because it's true."

She looked at me for about ten seconds sitting at that red light, not even breathing, it seemed. Then she turned away and didn't say a word, a blank expression on her face. It was the same thing she had done every other time I'd told her.

After our guys small group, Ron came up to me—the guy that I just wanted to sit and listen to him talk—and we had this great conversation about his past and the things he was learning. I liked him a lot. Then he turned the interrogation on me.

"Are you a believer, Jack?"

"No," I answered. Told him I was just there for Sara.

"Oh, okay—sorry, I was just curious." He took a drag off his cigarette.

"No reason to be sorry—I don't mind at all."

He blew out a puff of white smoke and smiled at me. "Jesus is after you though, isn't he?"

I looked at him, incredulous. But he couldn't possibly have meant it literally. Right? "I guess you could say that. But I don't think he's gonna catch me."

He grinned and blew a puff of smoke. "Yeah, I didn't think he was gonna catch me either." He threw his butt down and stepped on it. "Maybe you'll have better luck than I did."

49

Thanksgiving.

"Do you mind if I give thanks for our meal?" Yeshua asked. We were huddled around quite an incredible spread that he had been cooking up all day. I looked over at Sara, then back at him.

"No, go ahead."

"Okay." He bowed his head and was silent for a moment, so we followed suit.

"Father—" he paused. "Thank you for special new friends to share this holiday with. Thanks for providing for us and watching over us. Thank you for not only making food for our nourishment, but for making it taste so good, to remind us that you are good and that you are for our good. Thank you that you are peace and satisfaction for weary, hungry souls. Thank you." He paused. "So much. For everything. Amen."

I don't know how to explain this, but hearing his prayer was really powerful. I guess it was just the way he said it, the emotion in his voice—I don't know. But I remember thinking that I had never heard a prayer that sounded so much like there really was someone there on the other end of the line.

"Either of you want that turkey leg?" Sara asked. "Because if not, I'm about to crush it."

"Oh wow," I said, after taking a few bites in silence. "This is incredible."

"Yeah, it really is," said Sara. "Thanks so much, Yeshua."

"My pleasure," he said. "I'm just glad you are enjoying it."

"So where did you learn to cook?" I asked him.

"The Food Network," he said, and we both laughed.

I missed my family terribly that day, but it was still one of my favorite holidays in recent memory.

Yeshua came over on Saturday to watch the Clemson/South Carolina game with me. We were talking about it at Thanksgiving, and I was going on and on about how we'd had a rough season but we were going to pull off the upset. I just knew we were going to do it. I asked Yeshua who he was pulling for and he said he didn't really care, but that since I was a Clemson fan, he was going to pull for the Gamecocks.

I asked him if Jesus would do something like that.

He did. He showed up wearing a Gamecocks jersey, and I told him he was ridiculous.

I catch a lot of crap for being a Clemson fan living in Columbia.

"No using your magic God powers to smite me with a Clemson loss, okay?"

"I don't know what you're smoking sometimes. You think I really care who wins this game?" I told him I was just messing with him and laughed it off.

We had a lot of fun that day, despite Clemson getting killed. I don't want to talk about it. Next year...

Frank from Recovery called me that night. He said he had gotten into some trouble with his parents, and he was really pissed off because they took his car keys away from him. He called me because he was really wanting to use but was trying not to, and wanted to see if I wanted to hang out. I drove to pick him up at his house, and we went for a drive that ended up at the glorious Waffle House.

Glenda was there and she remembered me and said hello.

"So why are your parents pissed at you?"

"I came home messed up again the other night," he said. We sat in silence for a moment or two.

"So what do you think I should do?" he asked.

"You mean besides getting off drugs?"

He sat quiet for a minute. "I've tried man. I've tried."

"Frank—you shoot straight with me so I'm gonna shoot straight with you, okay?" He nodded his head. "Don't give me that bullshit. Don't give me your weary, 'life is so hard so I'm gonna give up' sad song. The fact is, you've got people that love you and support you, and they will do anything to help you get clean. There are people that walk away from drugs every day, and you can be one of them."

He didn't say anything for a minute, and then finally shook his head and said, "You're right."

"I know I'm right," I said, smiling at him. "Like always. It's a hard job, but somebody's got to do it."

"Whatever—" he said, shaking his head. "You know, Allen told me that at some point I'm going to have to get to a place where I believe Jesus is better than drugs. And that as long as I keep going back to drugs, whether I think it or not, deep down I believe that drugs are better."

"That makes a lot of sense," I said.

"So," he said, "do you believe Jesus is better than drugs?"

"Well—yeah. Jesus is better than drugs, Frank. I believe most anything is better than drugs. So pretty much anything would be a good trade."

"All right," he said after a moment. "Enough about my junk. What's up with you?" he asked. "And you can be real with me," he said. "I'm not a blabber mouth."

"I thought church people in the South are known for their gossip?"

"Not me, bro. We don't put up with that shit at Recovery." I laughed at him, then turned my coffee cup around a few times.

"All right."

He had been honest with me, after all. It's like you and me—I'm hoping you'll be straight with me since I'm telling you all of this about me.

"I had an affair with a girl from work. I broke it off but now my wife wants a divorce and she hardly lets me see my kids. She's dating this loser that I can't stand. And, let's not forget, we have a baby on the way, and I'm pushing thirty, sleeping in a spare bedroom at my little sister's apartment." I heaved an ironic smile at him.

"Wow," he said, eyes bugging out a bit. "I'm really sorry to hear about all that."

"Yeah, me too," I responded. "Me too. Like I said at Recovery the other night, I don't have any *serious* problems like you guys."

"Yeah," he said. "I can see that."

"Well," I said. "I hate it, but I don't think there is any changing it now. I think the last straw has fallen. I just hope I get good custody arrangements. But I probably won't."

"Hey—" he said, much harsher than normal, staring me down with a certain amount of ferocity. "Don't give me that 'things are hopeless so I'm gonna give up' sad violin bullshit. Your marriage is not over until the judge says it is. So fight for it, damn it."

I looked at him and held off tears.

"Yeah. You're right."

That night before I went to bed, I sent a text to Chloe:

Rivers and roads, Chloe. Rivers and roads. I'm not giving up on us.

50

We sat down for breakfast that Sunday morning and I immediately noticed that something was up with Yeshua. He just looked out of it. Like he was exhausted.

"What's up?" I asked him. "You look like you've been hit by a truck."

"Not quite," he said, trying to smile. "Just didn't sleep too well last night, I'll be fine. I'm sure this coffee will help."

I picked up my cup of coffee with both hands and said, "Ahh, coffee...our precious cure-all. What would we do without you?" I kissed my coffee cup and it made him laugh, then I said that I at least would have a major caffeine headache without you.

By the end of breakfast he seemed to be in a little better mood, so he tried to perk up and said, "All right Jack, let's go have some fun today. I don't know how much longer I'll be able to stick around."

I frowned at him and we both looked at each other for a long minute. Finally, he shot his eyes away from mine and down to the table. He asked me if I was ready and we got up and walked to the car without a word.

We arrived at some random church, and Yeshua put a roll of duct tape in his jacket before we walked in. I had no idea what was about to happen, but I was pretty excited.

We walked in, shook a few hands, then sat down. After a moment, he told me to stay put, that he would be back later, and walked off. The music started, and after a few minutes, he came back, did a weird half-smile at me, and plopped down in the pew beside me.

We sat through the rest of the church service and absolutely nothing happened. Yeshua just sat there, sometimes with his head in his hands—no stunt, nothing funny, nada. The preacher's sermon sounded similar to the televangelist we had seen, just not as overt, where it seemed like this business deal with God and he blesses you if you do good and punishes you if you screw up. He told some story from the Old Testament about the Israelites getting to the promised land, and kept talking about obeying God so we can get to our own promised land. People nodded their heads and took notes, and every time I glanced over at Yeshua during the service he just sat there and didn't look at me. I almost felt like he was pouting.

A few people spoke to us on the way out, and Yeshua was still quiet. I didn't really know what to say, so I asked him if he was hungry. We drove to the restaurant in almost complete silence and sat down at a table. I finally asked him what was wrong, said I thought we were going to pull some more antics.

"Jack, I'm sorry," he said, not looking at me. "I just didn't feel up to all that this morning. I couldn't bring myself to do it."

"What was the duct tape for?" I asked.

He shuffled in his seat a bit. "I was gonna go tape up the preacher and then preach my own little sermon—but I just couldn't do it."

I let it go and tried to make small talk while we decided what to order. That didn't go so well, so after we ordered I eventually decided to ask him the only question that came to my mind.

"So, Yeshua—Jesus, I have a question for you."

He looked up at me and exhaled, then told me to shoot.

"If this is not the way things work—if you don't make it a habit to show up to people and hang out with them like this, and this type of thing can't last forever like you said, then why me? Why do I get a burning bush if no one else does?"

He chewed on his lip for a moment, then looked me right in the eyes. "First and foremost, because I love you, Jack." He stopped to let that sink in. "And secondly, I wanted to help you see me through the mess of American Christianity. I wanted to help you see the truth about God through all of the hypocrisy, the pretense, the mistakes and failures of the church, and the wounds that you have endured."

We stared at each other for a while and didn't say anything. Finally, I broke the silence and asked him what he was going to say to that church this morning.

He thought for a minute and then looked up at me. "Do you remember that day at the cemetery? When you were asking me where I'd been all this time and why I hadn't stopped all the awful stuff that happened to you?"

"Yeah." I said. "I don't think I would forget that." I got kind of antsy.

He shook his head, like he was genuinely disgusted.

"I'm not kidding when I say the 'mess' of American Christianity. Prosperity teaching, this moralistic deism, business deal theology has soaked into the very fabric of Christianity somehow. And just like the things you said that night," he paused, "people believe that when bad things happen to them, that God is not keeping his end of the bargain. That he is betraying them, screwing them over. This Americanized God wants everyone to be wealthy, happy, prosperous and well-tanned, and if you'll just be good, then he'll keep anything bad from happening to you. He will make your business prosper. Your kids will be healthy and cool and successful. You'll have designer clothes. Everything will be comfortable and nice and peachy, your promised land will eventually come."

He stopped and swallowed, but didn't take his eyes away from mine.

"But what if your promised land—whatever you think that means—doesn't come? What if your kids get sick? What if you have a nightmare in your past that haunts you? What if you lose your job? What if your wife dies of cancer, and all of the 'promises' come crashing around you? What happens to you then?"

He leaned over the table toward me, intensity glaring in his eyes. It kind of scared me for a minute because he looked pissed.

"I'll tell you what happens. You get angry. You get really bitter deep down. You feel like you've been betrayed. Like God hasn't kept his end of the bargain. That he's a liar. Maybe you walk away from your faith. You didn't get what you wanted—what you thought you deserved. So God can't be trusted, and you're out.

"But what if I told you God never said those things? That there never was a business deal that would make your life perfect here on earth? That in fact, God says that things are going to be hard—really hard. That there is going to be pain, hardship, suffering, death and sickness and loss. That this is a desperately broken world because of sin. That he has promised to restore all things, to wipe sin and death and tears from the world and create a new heaven and earth for those reconciled to him. But that time is not here yet! Heaven will never be fully on earth because this is still a busted, sinful place." I had never seen him like this, so my eyes were glued to him with an intensity that matched his.

"There is no quicker way to become angry and bitter than believing things about God that he has never said about himself. And what's worse, when people do this, they are treating God like a genie in a bottle. Three wishes and he gives you what you want. It's essentially turning God into a product. The cosmic vending machine of the American dream. A means to an end, a measly errand boy to fetch what you really want.

"But he is not a personal magic genie to make you rich and successful. He is not your rabbit's foot or your good luck charm or the next product to get what you want in life. He is God, and you've been taught to treat him like a butler! A self-help product to get you a better marriage, a better financial portfolio, or a more prosperous life.

"And here is the saddest part: not only are people trusting in lies that will leave them bitter and angry—they are looking right past the real thing to the fool's gold. They are missing the truth—" He inhaled deeply, then let all the air out.

"You get God! Don't you see? You get him! *He* is the promised land! *He* is the reward! *He* is the prize! The giver that people prostitute is the gift! You get *him*…you get him to be there with you when bad things happen. You get his peace when you lose your job or when someone gets really sick. You get his presence—his presence that tells you no matter how bad things are, that he is there, that he knows, that he's got you. You get to hear him say that he hates these effects of sin as much as you do, and that he is making all things new. God offers you something better than that pipe dream—he offers you himself. His presence through everything. There is no promised land without God—you could have every good thing that exists, but you'd still be miserable without him." He looked like he was about to tear up and I sat completely still.

"In the cross, God has proven once and for all that he is good and that he is for your good. No circumstance of life can ever change that. God's goodness is not dependent on your circumstances, and faithfulness does not magically guarantee external blessings or an easy, comfortable life. It may very well bring hardship and persecution—something the American church knows nothing about."

I exhaled and he shook his head in some mixture of despair and disgust. "All of those people this morning," he said, "well-meaning, everyday people who are being misled by these false beliefs. It's an epidemic. An epidemic." He said the word slowly, drawing out the syllables the second time. "The theology of suffering in most of American Christianity is pretty pathetic."

Right about then the waitress brought our food and I was relieved to get a breath. As we started to eat, I decided to poke him a little.

"So, the good news is that I get you, through good times and bad, and you'll never leave me or forsake me. Except for the small fact," I said, paused, then went on, "that pretty soon here, you are going to leave me and forsake me."

He dropped his fork on his plate, put his napkin on the table and I could have sworn he started crying.

I quickly got up and went to the restroom to give us both a minute.

I looked in the mirror in the bathroom and said, "What the hell did you say that for?"

When I got back to the table, he was eating again. So I said, what else is wrong with American Christianity, now that we're on the topic. He still looked unsettled and asked me how much time I had. I told him all day. He started to spew out this rant…and I mean *rant*. He said some churches need to take field trips to local bars to learn how to be family, then talked about Christians not being generous and sacrificial with money—churches spending loads of money on insanely lavish buildings instead of giving more to missions and helping meet genuine needs in the world. He said the American church has so much potential to change the world but wastes so much on themselves in this consumeristic vortex.

I told him some horror stories about waiting tables in college on Sundays. Church people in the South really are the worst tippers. It's so bad that at the restaurant where I worked, they had to force us to work Sundays because nobody wanted to. The worst was when people left those fake twenty-dollar bill tracts and not even a penny. I kid you not. Talk about making a waiter furious.

He paid for our meal that day with a hundred-dollar bill and when the waitress came back with our change he told her to keep it. She was a young pregnant girl and she was very taken aback when he said that.

"Are you serious?" she asked.

"Yep. You did a great job. And you need to start saving for him, or her—" She reached down, touched her belly and grinned.

"Thank you so much," she said. "I can't say how much I appreciate that." After a second she left, still shell-shocked. He took a pen out of his pocket and scribbled something on a napkin in front of the menu holder between us. When we got up to leave I looked to see what it said. It read: *You are insanely loved by God. Good luck with your baby.*

51

Around 5 pm that Sunday afternoon, Luis called me. "Hey buddy, how you?"

"I'm good, Luis, how are you?"

"I still alive *ese*! That's good."

"Yeah, I guess it is," I said, laughing.

"Listen buddy, I ask you a favor. We do a food drive at church, and I got some stuff to take, but I can't carry it all and walk. You stay near me, I know, so I wonder, you can take me there tonight?"

I hesitated, trying to come up with a good excuse. He started backing out after a few seconds of silence, saying that he'd just walk and figure it out. I let out a frustrated spew of expletives in my mind. "No, I can take you Luis…no problem. What time should I pick you up?"

"6:30," he said. "Hehe. Thanks buddy."

We pulled into the parking lot and I helped him carry the bags of food into the foyer of the building. We stepped back outside and I told Luis that I would see him later.

"What? You not stay?"

"No, I need to run some errands, but I can come back and pick you up though."

"No…" he said, furrowing his dark brow. "Come on, stay." Some people were walking outside from the previous service now, and others starting to arrive. Before I could respond to Luis, I felt someone tap me on the shoulder.

"Jack!" he said when I turned around. "I didn't expect to see you here!"

"Yea I was just—" he leaned in to hug me and cut me off. "It's good to see you, Edmond."

"Yes, brother, it's good to see you too. How is Sara?"

I told him she was doing okay, I guess. I was starting to get a little claustrophobic from the people passing by. I wanted to leave.

"Look who it is," Edmond said, turning away from me. Frank strolled up to our little circle and we all said hey to him. He pulled out a cigarette and lit it up. By that time Ron had come down the stairs. He walked over to us, smiling.

"Well if it isn't the Brady Bunch," he said. "Good to see you fellas. Jack, great to see you here." I told him likewise, and he asked Frank for a cigarette. He rested on his walker and reached into his pocket to get them out, then handed the pack to Ron, along with a lighter. I stood there and wondered if there had ever been a more eclectic, interesting group of people standing outside of a church service smoking.

Right then Willie walked up and saw us, then made a beeline over to where we were standing. He was carrying a large cardboard box on his right shoulder.

"Willie!" someone said. Ron asked him what was in the box.

He plunked the box down in the middle of our circle, then stood up straight to pop his back. "I'm gon' show you," he said. He bent down and opened the box, then pulled out a white t-shirt and held it scrunched in his hands. He looked around at all of us, then said, "This here is what you call a new fashion trend. This is the official Willie shirt." With that he popped the shirt out straight and we all doubled over laughing. Plastered across the front was a huge drawing of his face. Derby hat on his head with his bottom lip poked out. He started giggling too. "You know it's awesome," he went on.

"You know you want one." We all moved in closer to admire it.

"Only ten dollars a piece," he said. "Aside from what it cost, one dollar goes to the Children's Hunger Fund, to help feed those kids who don't have no food. Fifty cents goes to our family, Midtown Fellowship, and the rest of the profit goes to help start my new business."

Edmond asked him what his new business was, and he looked at us like it was obvious. "Willie Shirt," he said. "Willie Shirt dot com." We all laughed. "I'm serious," he said, still grinning. "So who wants one? Jack, I know you want one. Look how good it will look on you." He held one up to my chest.

"Well…" I said. "Willie, you're right. That is awesome. I absolutely want one." I started getting out my wallet and he grinned and reached his long, bony arm into the box. I bought a white one from him, and right about then a guy around my age walked up to us and started laughing. "Dustin," Ron said. "This is our friend Jack, have you met him yet?"

"I don't believe I have," he said, stepping over to me. "Nice to meet you, Jack." I said likewise and turned to shake his hand.

"Dustin is the one who helped start our crazy family," Ron said. "He's got a tough job putting up with all of us, that's for sure. But he loves it. Don't you, Dustin?"

"Yep," he said, shaking his head. "It's good to have you, Jack. I see you are already fitting in pretty well," he said, pointing to the white shirt draped over my shoulder.

"Yeah," I said, laughing. "Willie has quite the style."

"Yeah, I've got a blue one at home," Dustin said. "I thought about preaching in it but I didn't want Willie to get a big head." He winked at Willie, who was smiling and showing his missing teeth.

"I think it's a little too late for that…judging from those shirts," Frank said. Everyone laughed.

"Nuh uh," Willie said. "I ain't got no big head…"

"You better not, Willie," Dustin said. "I'm preaching about pride tonight and I'd hate to have to humble you." He smiled and fake punched Willie in the stomach. Willie jerked back and went into a fake boxing pose for a second.

"I'm already humble," Willie said. "I'm so humble I don't even know how to describe it."

52

That Tuesday night Luis invited me over to his house for dinner. I guess he wanted to repay me for taking him to church that week.

"*Hola amigo*!" He acted like I was the president when he opened the door. "So good to see you! Come in, come in."

He shared the transitional house with a few other formerly homeless guys, but they weren't there that night. The living room looked like a college dorm, and the TV was blaring the Spanish channel.

He was still cooking so I walked in the kitchen and asked if I could help. He told me no, that I could sit at the table. He already had a place set for me with a paper plate and plastic cup.

"You want some water, buddy?" I told him yes and he grabbed my cup off of the table and put it under the faucet, no ice, then brought it back to me.

"Sorry, I forget to get *hielo*." I remember just enough Spanish to get me by. I said no problem and put the cup up to my mouth to drink the lukewarm water.

He finished up and started bringing stuff over. Steak tacos, with authentic Mexican tortillas and homemade chopped pico. It looked quite good. "Luis, this looks delicious. I wish you wouldn't have went all out like this." I felt bad, thinking about how little work and money he had.

"Nonsense!" He furled his big bushy eyebrows at me. "I want to." We dug in, and it was very good. Lime juice absolutely makes a steak taco.

"Uh-oh!" he said. "We forget to pray…" He crossed his hands, elbows on table, and bowed his head. "God, we thank you for dis day. We thank you for dis food. I thank you for my friend Jack. Amen! Hehe…"

After a few minutes he asked about my family, and how things were going with the wife. I told him that they were pretty much the same, that Chloe was still very mad at me. He told me that he understood, that he knew marriage could be hard. The whole time I was talking he sat there and nodded his head, like he didn't care about anything in the world except what I was telling him. I did smell alcohol on his breath, though, so I wondered if I should ask him about it.

"Luis, have you been drinking today?"

He frowned and got a pained look on his face. "Yeah, I do," he said. "But only a few. I not drunk." He was quiet for a moment. "Thanks for asking."

"Of course. Just trying to be a friend," I said. "You have to be careful with that stuff when you have a problem with it."

"Yeah, you right," he said. "I know."

"So you want to tell me your story?"

"Yeah," he answered, shaking his head again. "My wife left me seven years ago. She took my two daughters, Yasmine and Brenda, with her. I not seen them since." His voice quivered a little just saying that, and I could tell it was still a fresh wound.

"You see my tattoo?" He rolled up his shirt sleeve, and pointed to his arm. There was a large cursive Y and B, with the rest of their names spelled out in a much smaller font.

"Oh yeah. I like that." I wasn't sure what to say.

He still looked at his arm.

"They are *mi hijas*. My sweet daughters. I miss them so much."

"I'm sure you do, Luis. I'm so sorry about that."

"Probly I not the best father to them. But I love them." I nodded my head, thinking of how I could change the topic to something not so sad.

"So do you have other family around?"

"Nah—brothers and sisters in Oklahoma. I talk to them on the phone, but I never see them. It's expensive, you know." I nodded my head. "I send them money when I can. I'm about to be a *tio*...hehe!" He waved his arm in the air, really excited.

"*Tio*?"

"Mmm...uncle. My sister—she's having a baby!"

"Congratulations!" He said thanks and still beamed.

We talked a while longer, and then he looked at me serious, and said, "Buddy—Jack, I just want you to know something. If you need to talk to somebody, about anything, you can talk to me, okay?" I told him okay and thanked him. "I serious," he went on. "I a good listener—" he laughed at himself, then got serious again. "I want to be your friend."

"Thanks Luis. I want to be your friend too."

We finished up dinner and moved to the living room. We sat there for an hour watching some comedy show. I didn't understand anything, but he giggled and laughed like it was the funniest thing he'd ever seen. And I laughed with him.

53

Wednesday night Chloe agreed to let me watch the boys at the house while she went to her book club. When I walked in, I instantly realized how much I missed the way my house smelled.

"Daddy daddy daddy daddy!" The boys jumped all around me, and I went to the playroom with them after Chloe left. Isaac pulled on my hand when we got in there, and almost broke my heart: "Daddy, don't leave."

I don't know how I didn't cry. "I didn't leave, buddy—I've just been busy. I love you." I looked down at his huge blue eyes.

"I love you too, Daddy." He wrapped his arms around my leg and I cringed.

I am so thankful that kids are so forgiving, and that they have such short memories.

We played for a while and I had a blast with them, but then it was time for bed. I put them down a little early so I'd have time to prepare everything.

After they were asleep, I got my bag of goodies out of the car, and started spreading rose pedals from the doorway into the living room. I got out candles and several framed pictures of us, and decorated the room with them. I got my iPod hooked up to the speakers, ready to play "All My Life" by K-Ci and Jo-Jo. It was our first dance at our wedding.

Ridiculous, I know.

I had written out notes on big index cards, and I taped them to the wall, one after another from the hallway to the living room.

I'm sorry for being such a moron. I don't deserve you.
I promise I will never, ever betray you again.

I'm sorry for failing our family.
I promise to be the most dedicated husband and father ever.

I'm sorry that Donnie Clark looks like a good option to you right now.
I promise that if I get the chance I will be so much better than him.

I'm sorry that you don't know if you can trust me anymore.
I promise I will earn that trust back and more if you will let me.

I'm sorry that I am miserable at being romantic.
I promise that I will step up my game. Big time.

I'm sorry for not treating you like the princess you are.
I promise I am different now. Completely different.

I'm sorry that I don't deserve a second chance.
I promise that if you give me one I will never let you down again.

Rivers and roads, babe. Rivers and roads.
I won't stop at anything to try to win you back.

I finished getting ready, then went up to check on the boys. They were sound asleep, so I went back downstairs, sat on the couch and waited. Twenty or thirty minutes went by as I stood, sat, stood, paced and repeated. Finally, I heard Chloe's car pull up in the driveway. I stood up, pressed play on my iPod playlist, smoothed out my pants, and my mouth got really dry and bad-tasting.

I forgot to tell you I put my best suit on.

A decade passed (at least it seemed), and she opened the front door. The candlelight drew her gaze and she looked very confused.

"Jack, what's going on? Where are the boys?"

"Upstairs asleep—they are fine. Just come on in." She hesitated, then stepped in far enough to close the door. Slowly walking this way, she crossed her arms and squinted to read the index cards, still looking confused. Guess I could have written them on something bigger, huh? She stepped forward, reading each one in turn. After about the fourth one, I could tell something was happening. Maybe, just maybe, I was getting through.

I got a little soppy-eyed too, and she finished reading the cards and quietly stepped into the living room, looking down at the floor. K-Ci and Jo-Jo were doing their job, and doing it well.

"Do you remember this song?"

"Of course, Jack." She was full-on crying now, and she reached up to wipe her face. I reached and gave her a tissue. She looked around the room, half-smiling at some of the pictures.

"Chloe, I genuinely cannot tell you how sorry I am for how my actions have hurt you. Words are so shallow compared to what I wish I could express to you. I promise you that I have woken up from my slumber of stupidity, and I am a different man now. I will never take you for granted again if you will give me another chance. The man that you married all those years ago is back, and I love you so much more than I ever have." I exhaled and paused.

"I want to share this house with you and raise our boys and our little one on the way together—to make more memories than we could ever remember. I want to hold you and protect you and make the bed warm for you at night. I want to be your prince again, and I will do anything to prove that to you. I promise."

She huffed and sniffled a little, then looked away. "It's a girl," she said through the tears.

"A girl," I repeated, smiling and heaving forward a little. "Marley."

"Yeah," she said, with a trembling exasperation. "Marley."

"I hope she looks just like you."

She said nothing. Just stood there, motionless, looking at the same spot in the floor. Tears fell from her face to the carpet. A painfully silent moment went by. The first song ended and "Rivers and Roads" started playing next.

"I'll do anything in the world you ask me to do," I went on. "I'll get on my knees and beg—I will do anything." She still stood unmoving, head in hands. "I miss you, Chloe. I miss you like hell." She was more beautiful than I can describe, the candlelight lighting her figure afire.

"So what do you think, honey? I'm not asking to move back in now or anything like that. But will you consider giving me a second chance? To at least work toward being together again?"

She took a step back, then her eyes came up to meet mine. They winced, birthing a few more tears.

"Rivers and roads, huh?" she asked, looking straight into my eyes.

"Rivers and roads," I said, quickly and confidently. "Or mountains, valleys, oceans, and deserts. I don't care. I'll do anything to get you back. Anything. Please."

She stood there silently and rocked back and forth on her heels. She wiped her nose on her sleeve and looked at me. Like she was trying to look inside of me somehow, to see if any of the man she once loved was still there.

After a minute, the song got to the best part where the girl is singing that haunting chorus over and over again at the end, and Chloe suddenly stepped over to the stereo and turned the music off. Everything went silent and I shifted my feet like I was hovering on eggshells.

"I need you to clean this mess up and leave." There was a cold desperation in her voice. She gazed at me for another moment, then turned away and went up the stairs.

Tears fell down my anguished face, and I picked my bruised heart up off the floor and followed her upstairs. Halfway up she turned around to face me and told me again to clean up the mess and leave.

I threw away the last hopes for my marriage with those rose petals that night.

54

What a frustrating thing language is.

I felt like if I could just explain myself to her, if I could just somehow show her how sorry and serious I was, how I was different on the inside now, that she would surely take me back. She would see the old me there, the man she loved and married, and she would want to at least try. But there is only so much that words can convey, unfortunately.

If I knew Chloe, that was the last straw. Again, it was her eyes. They said we were done.

Sometimes you only get that one shot. One speech.

I got mine and it, like so much else in my life, was a miserable failure.

When I got back to the apartment that night, Yeshua was waiting on me. I got out of the car and he was sitting on the steps. He stood up and looked at me with a question mark on his face. He could tell what happened the second he saw me.

"Come on, let's go for a drive," he said.

I just handed him my keys, because I didn't want to drive. I got in the passenger side and slumped down in my seat.

We didn't say a word in the car, and he stopped at a gas station to fill up my car because I was on empty. When he came out of the store he had two tall boy Newcastles in a brown paper bag.

He lifted them up and half-smiled at me. "You up for going to the river and sitting for a while?"

I still said nothing, but nodded my head in agreement.

We arrived at the river, bundled up, then walked to sit on a park bench and opened our beers. We sat there for, I don't know, an hour maybe, in complete silence. *It's over...she's done* kept running through my mind, and part of me wanted to say it out loud, but I knew if I did I would erupt into a blubbering mess. So, I didn't. The soothing rush of the river calmed me down a little bit, and I tried to focus on it and just listen. I finished my beer and twirled the bottle in my hands for a bit, then sat it down below my feet. But after another minute, something came over me and I stood up, grabbed the bottle and threw it out in the river as far as I could. It made it to this concrete barrier and shattered. I don't know—it was stupid. I just felt the need to throw something, so I did.

We sat for a while longer, and then Yeshua leaned over and put his hand on my shoulder and squeezed. He left it there for a bit without speaking, then he slowly opened his mouth. "Jack...I just want you to know that I love you. And that I am so sorry tonight didn't turn out better."

I didn't say anything at first, for a few minutes. Finally, I worked up the will to respond. "Thanks," I said, then paused. "Thanks for the beer. And thanks for not giving me a pep talk tonight."

"You're welcome," he said, then shifted in his seat a bit. "Sometimes silence is much more appropriate than words."

After a while, he drove me back to Sara's. I opened up her medicine cabinet that night, and I'm not sure what I took, but I didn't make it to work on Thursday morning.

55

Allen came up to me before Recovery on Thursday to check on Sara. I told him that I was really worried about her this week. She seemed extra down and zombie-like, and had worn long sleeves all week. I asked to see her wrists several times but she refused. He asked if we needed to do something more drastic, like try to get her committed somewhere, but I told him there was no way she'd agree to that. So he told me he'd talk to her small group leader and see if she could talk to her one-on-one.

That night Allen talked about something he called Christian hedonism, which is basically all the stuff that Yeshua told me—seeking satisfaction in God. He even read one of the same passages that Yeshua quoted from Psalm 107, which I thought was weird. But I thought that it does make a lot of sense to teach people in Recovery that chasing God is better than drugs or pornography or whatever it is they deal with.

On the way home that night Sara told me that she wasn't going back to Recovery no matter what I did or threatened her with.

"Why?" I pleaded with her.

"Because they tried to make me talk tonight. I don't want to talk. There's nothing to talk about."

That was when I started to really worry about her.

Friday afternoon, I stopped at Starbucks in Five Points to get some coffee to go, and on my way out I noticed Willie sitting on a bench across the street.

I thought for a minute, then walked over to him.

"Willie, what's up?"

"Oh, hey Jack." He reached up and shook my hand, smiling. "What you doing?"

"Just grabbing some coffee real quick. What are you doing?"

"Oh, you know. Just sitting." He twiddled his thumbs, looking down.

"I thought you told me that you needed to stay away from Five Points? Are you getting into trouble down here?"

"I told you that?" he asked, looking up at me.

"Yeah, you did. On the way home from Recovery that night. Remember?"

"Oh," he said, thinking. "I did, didn't I?" He didn't say anything for a few minutes. I guess he thought if he ignored the question it would go away. Finally, I asked him if he wanted me to take him somewhere. He thought for a minute, then slapped his knees and looked at me. "Yeah, that would be good. You can take me to the Vista?" I told him yes and we walked to my car just in time to see a meter maid writing me a ticket.

"Rhonda…" Willie said.

"Oh, hey, Willie," she responded, smiling. He launched into a spiel of sweet-talking, telling her that I was his friend and I was helping him out, and asked her to please not give me a ticket. She looked at him and then me, smiled, and tore the ticket up. "Y'all have a nice day," she said, walking away.

On the way Willie asked to borrow my phone, and I gave it to him.

"I need to call Adam," he said, punching in the number.

"Hey, Adam—it's Willie. Hey, you at the office? Okay. Can I come by there for a while and hang out? I was down in Five Points about to get into trouble, but my friend Jack picked me up. Okay, thanks. We'll be there soon."

He hung up the phone and handed it back to me.

"Thanks, Jack. For real."

"No problem Willie."

"You know," he said, looking at me and grinning. "You aight. You aight, Jack…"

"You know, you're all right too, Willie." He let out a raspy, high-pitched laugh that made me want to laugh too.

56

That Saturday Chloe agreed to let me have the boys for the day, so we went to the park to have a picnic and play. We sat down and spread out our lunch to eat, and soon after Yeshua came walking up. I had told him he could join us if he wanted, and he was really excited about it.

"Issac, Liam, look. This is my friend, Yeshua."

"Hey boys! It's so nice to meet you." He bent down to his knees and rubbed both of their heads. They both had a mouth full of food but looked up at him and smiled.

"Can you say Yeshua?" I asked them. Liam tried to say it and actually got pretty close. It was funny.

After we ate, the boys wanted to play football. Yeshua brought a ball, so we decided to play—me and Isaac versus Yeshua and Liam. We marked off the boundaries with our shoes and played. The kids being two and all, there weren't a lot of rules—that kind of stuff is so much fun with kids their age. We mostly just played everything up to make the boys laugh and let it end in a tie so neither of them would pout. What can I say—Bennetts have the sore loser gene.

We were pretty disgusting afterward, so I decided to take the boys back to the apartment to get cleaned up. I cleaned up all of our stuff and my hands were pretty full, so the boys both grabbed one of Yeshua's hands to walk across the street to our car. He helped me get them in the car and told both of them that he had fun playing with them and that we'd have to do it again sometime.

He told Liam good job tackling me, and Liam gave him a high five. I got in the car and asked Yeshua if he wanted a ride but he turned quickly and said no, that he needed to go, and he walked away in the opposite direction while we drove home. He seemed angry, or sad, and I didn't know what to say.

That was the beginning of the end.

That night after I took the boys back home, I was being lazy around the apartment, watching TV. Then my phone rang. It was an unknown number, but I was just lonely enough to pick it up.

"Jack—Jack, it's Yeshua." I knew immediately that something was wrong.

"What's up?" I said. "What's wrong?"

"Can you come down here and meet me?"

"Come meet you where?" I asked.

"At The Whig," he said. "At our favorite booth."

I told him I'd be right there. I couldn't tell for sure, but from the way he sounded on the phone I thought he was...*drunk*?

Impossible.

57

He was plastered.

I sat down across from him and didn't say anything for a minute. "Jack," he said like he had been waiting on me for years. "You made it. Thank you."

"What's going on?" I said.

He got the hint that I was pissed and started turning his beer mug around on the table. Then, his eyes got really watery and a few tears escaped. He looked at me and winced. I hated him and somehow felt sorry for him at the same time.

"I've got something to tell you, Jack."

"Yeah, really?" I said. "Lemme guess—you're not really Jesus, Son of God, from the Bible, in the flesh, my own personal guardian angel."

"I'm sorry," he finally said.

"Yeah," I said. "I'm sorry too."

I mean, I knew all along that he wasn't the real Jesus. But I'd be lying if I said part of me didn't want him to be. And now that our little game was over, I felt stupid and angry and taken advantage of.

My best friend suddenly felt like my worst enemy.

He put his forehead down on the table and started to cry. I told him to get up and stop it, then I went and ordered him a burger to help him sober up. And I got us both a glass of water.

He drank the water like he was dying of thirst, and I just sat there staring at him, feeling pulled in a dozen different directions.

"So how many have you had?" I asked.

He started to count on his fingers, then put them down. "Too many."

"So," I said, "now that our little song and dance is over, I think you owe me some answers."

He sat back and wiped his mouth with his sleeve, then swallowed and thought for a second. "Well, we have two options," he said, head still wobbly.

"Is one of them to punch you in the face?" I asked, only half-joking.

"Make that three options," he said, putting up three fingers. I shook my head and told him to go on.

"The first option is," he said, "that I will walk out of that door right now and you will never ever see me again. I lied to you and you probably hate me. You should. So I'll just disappear forever and you can forget about me. And you can punch me in the face first if you want to." More tears were coming to his eyes, and he exhaled a loud sense of disappointment.

"Okay. And option number two?"

"Option number two," he said. "Option number two is—"

At that moment, my phone buzzed on the table, and I glanced down to see that it was a text from Sara.

Jack, I am so sorry. I just couldn't hold on anymore. I love you and I always have. Don't give up on Chloe and tell the boys I love them.

My heart pounded in my ears like a drum in slow motion. I half-yelled some expletive and started to get up.

"Wait!" Yeshua said, grabbing my arm.

"Get off me!" I yelled and shoved his hand away.

"What is it?" he asked, and I told him, Sara's in trouble.

I ran outside to my car as fast as I could, and I could feel Yeshua stumbling behind me. I tried to leave without him, but he started pounding on my passenger-side window something fierce. I don't have time for this, I thought, but I couldn't just leave him.

I reached over and let him in.

58

We barreled into the front door of the apartment. "Sara! Sara!" I screamed, running all over the apartment. "Sara!" I checked her room first, then noticed the bathroom door was closed. I almost knocked it down getting in there.

All I could see was her phone lying in the floor beside the bathtub. I ran forward to see her limp body lying face up in the tub, box cutters in her right hand and blood still gushing from both of her wrists.

Everything was *red*.

"Sara…" I heaved with a giant sob.

Yeshua stepped in front of me and knocked me on the ground to get to her. He bent down, put his arms around her body, and pulled her up to his chest.

We ran to my car as fast as we could. I got in the driver's seat and he sat holding her across his body in the passenger seat, blood all over his face and clothes and everywhere. We were both sobbing, and Sara's pale face rested on his shoulder.

"Sara! Sara!" I kept yelling, over and over, begging her to answer. She was cold and unconscious, turning bluer by the minute. Yeshua grabbed both of her wrists where she was bleeding and wrapped his hands around the cuts to try to stop the gushing blood. He sobbed and kept repeating, God, no; God, no—the tears running down his cheeks mixing with Sara's blood.

I screeched to a halt at the ER door and left the car running. Inside, they took us straight back to the trauma bay. He carried her until they put out a white bed for us to lay her down on. The sheets turned red instantly as her body hit them, and doctors surrounded her.

We stepped back and into that helpless state where you can do nothing more but weep or pray, and a nurse came up to us with a clipboard. "What happened?" She looked at me.

"We found her in the bathtub with her wrists slit and got her here as fast as we could," I whimpered. "Can you save her?"

"We will do everything we can." Her words sounded so shallow and insignificant. "I promise," she added, which wasn't comforting. "You are…?"

"Her brother," I said.

"And who are you?" she said, turning to Yeshua.

He was almost unrecognizable. Painted in burgundy, chest still heaving with sobs.

"I'm her father," he finally said. "Yancey Bennett."

59

"Get the hell out of here," I said, voice trembling. "Get out of here right now—I don't have time for this."

I was sitting in the waiting room—Chloe was on her way—and he was standing in front of me. I didn't dare look him in the eyes, whoever he was. I just wanted him to leave, or maybe die. My head rested in my hands and I stared at my blood-spattered shoes.

After saying he wasn't leaving this time, and a few minutes of me ignoring him, he turned and sat down several seats away.

It wasn't far enough away for me.

Eventually, Chloe came running in with the boys and she came straight to hug me. I held her so tightly—I know I got blood all over her clothes, but it was the most comforting thing in the world.

Finally I let go of her, just as Liam spotted the man who was pretending to by my father. He raised his hand and tried to say "Hey, Yeshua." Yeshua smiled at him and waved.

"Who is that?" Chloe asked me.

"He's nobody," I said, and sat back down in the corner.

I brought the boys up on my lap and held them while Chloe asked a bunch of questions I didn't know the answers to.

We sat and waited for five miserable eternities it seemed. Chloe occasionally glanced over at Yeshua to try to figure out what was going on, but I just totally ignored him.

Then, without warning, the doctor pushed open the door and walked in. The entire world went completely silent and still, and a sound similar to white noise buzzed in my ear, I assume from the overload of exhaustion and despair.

We all stood up straight and inhaled. The doctor opened her mouth and did that pause like they do on TV—the one that bad news usually follows. I held my breath.

"She is very unstable and has lost a lot of blood," she started. "But we got her back for now." There was a collective sigh in the room and we all cried. The best news I had ever heard in my life. "We are nowhere near out of the woods yet and will have to see how she does," she continued. "But we are hoping she will be okay."

I let out a heaping wave of air from my chest, and turned to plead with the doctor. "Can I see her?"

"No, not right—"

"Please," I interrupted. "Please."

She tightened her mouth. "Give us a minute. I'll come back for you."

After I calmed down a bit, I told Chloe I'd be right back and walked over to where Yeshua was sitting. I sat down with an empty chair between us and turned so that Chloe couldn't see me. "Okay," I said to him. "You know Sara is okay now. I still don't know who you are, but I do know two things. The first is that I never want to see you again, and the second is that you don't belong here." He grimaced and I bored my eyes into his. "Leave," I said, gritting my teeth. "Right now. If you don't I am going to physically fight you right here. Not kidding." He went to stand up, his face betraying nothing, looked at me one last time, and slowly walked away and out the door without looking back.

After I went back to Chloe she asked me again who that was. I told her it was a long story and that I didn't want to talk about it.

A nurse finally came to get us and we left the boys with her while we walked back to see Sara. There she was, unconscious and restful, chest heaving up and down with the oxygen machine. Her wrists were bandaged up tightly, blood pumping into my right forearm. The heart rate machine beeped slowly, but steadily. I bent down and kissed her on her forehead, rubbing my fingers through her wet hair.

My precious, baby sister.

60

Within thirty minutes of Yeshua's departure, Allen showed up. He poked his head in the waiting room like he didn't want to disturb us. I saw him and told Chloe I'd be back. I told him to follow me and we walked a ways away to a quiet hallway.

"Allen," I said, stopping and turning to him. "What are you doing here?"

"Yancey just called me and told me everything so I raced here."

"'Yancey'? Seriously? Don't lie to me," I said, "please. Who is he really?"

"Jack, I don't know," he said. "I know him as Yancey Bennett. All I know is that a few years ago he got out of jail and that he was in for a long time. And that he's been at Recovery for alcohol abuse for a while now. He disappeared the last few months and none of us saw him. We knew nothing about him meeting you or what he was telling you about who he was—I swear."

"My father has been dead for a long time. I don't know what kind of prank he's playing. What kind of person would pretend to be your dead father? Or *Jesus*? Is he crazy?"

"Jack, I don't know, and I'm not saying he's your father. I'm just telling you what I know." I stood with my arms crossed, trying to make sense out of everything. "I will leave if you want me to Jack, just tell me. Or I can stay. Whatever you want."

I stared at him for a minute, then told him no, that he could stay. He asked if it was okay to invite some other people from Recovery to come and I said yes. We walked back into the waiting room and I introduced him to Chloe.

Within an hour Luis showed up. Then, a few of the girls from Recovery. Then Ron, and Frank a bit later. Luis sat and played with the boys while the rest of us talked. I got to go see Sara one more time and she was still out, but breathing steady. It was so comforting to stand and watch her chest rise and fall.

It was getting really late, so after a while people slowly started going home. Chloe stayed until almost everyone was gone, but then left to get the boys in bed. Luis and Frank offered to spend the night there with me and I told them to go home, but they insisted on staying.

Later that night she woke up for a few minutes.

"Sara? Sara, are you awake?" Her eyes flittered open, then closed, then open again. She still had the tube in her throat and couldn't talk.

Her eyes became soggy and a few tears escaped as she realized where she was. "Honey, everything is okay," I told her. "You are gonna be fine." She slowly grabbed my hand and opened it, then used her index finger to spell something on my palm. She spelled SORRY.

"It's okay sweetheart, it's okay," I said. "I love you, Sara." She nodded and closed her eyes again as I squeezed her hand and bent down to kiss her again. I stood there and brushed her bangs off of her forehead and held her hand until she went to sleep again.

She stayed in the hospital for a few days, slowly getting better and better. I didn't leave once, and they were nice enough to let me shower there. Chloe came and went but stayed as long as she could, and the people from Recovery literally acted like my family. At least one of them were there at all times it seemed, and they got to go back and see her a good bit.

I took Luis back to see her for the first time one of those days, and he gave her a homemade card that he had made for her. It was a piece of normal white computer paper, folded in half with balloons drawn all over it in different colors. On the inside, in big, scribbled letters it said: I PRAY YOU BETTER SARA!!! LOVE, YOUR AMIGO LUIS.

He smiled so wide when he gave it to her. Her eyes glistened and she told him thank you and gave him a one-armed hug.

61

Sara slowly improved that week, and the hospital discharged her into a behavioral health hospital.

The apartment got some kind of lonely that next week. A few times I went to plug in at a coffee shop for a bit, just so I could hear other people type and sip and laugh. The whir of the espresso machine. You know. Sometimes you just want to have another human around, to hear someone else breathe, because it seems to make things feel like they are not as bad as they are.

As you would probably guess, I drank a lot that week.

Yes, everyone from Recovery called and texted a lot. An annoying amount, actually. I ignored them all. Don't get me wrong, I was thankful for everything they had done. I just didn't want to talk to them at the time.

One night when I was drunk, I wrote a letter to him. I don't remember exactly what it said, but I know it was the meanest thing I have ever said or probably ever thought. I remember saying that I wished he would kill himself in the middle of the woods where he wouldn't be found, so his body would be lonely and "un-mourned" for dozens of years. I don't think un-mourned is even a word, but I was drunk so who cares? Anyway, it was really bad.

Thursday night I went to see Sara during visiting hours. I sat there with her in this little white room, with a few lockers and some uncomfortable blue chairs lining the wall.

"You enjoying your stay here at the luxurious Three Rivers?" I asked her.

"Yes, yes, quite enjoyable," she said. "It's wonderful being locked up and forced to eat terrible food and talk about your problems all day. Just wonderful." I laughed at her and told her that things could be worse. She asked how and I said some ridiculous stuff like blindfolded parallel parking or hosting a reality TV show.

She asked me about the apartment, Chloe, and the boys. She was certain that the place was a mess and I assured her my marriage was still a mess, too.

"Are you gonna be okay, big brother?" She half-smiled at me, genuinely concerned. It felt really good to have her care enough to ask me that.

"I think so," I said. "I hope so." I paused and studied the room. "The more important question is: are you gonna be okay, little sis?"

She looked me in the eye. For the first time since I can remember. "I hope so," she said.

"I hope so too," I said, looking at her. "You're the only family I have left—you better not leave me here alone, you hear me?" She just looked back at me and gave me a sad smile.

We sat together for a minute without saying much, and it was one of my favorite moments ever with Sara. I felt closer to her than I ever had before. And suddenly, in the midst of all my insides bubbling, I decided that I had to tell her. I just had to.

So I tell her everything.

And then she starts this cold, blank stare at the wall and doesn't budge her eyes for a solid minute. Finally, she looks up at me and asks, "Have you seen him since?"

"No. I don't plan to ever see him again. I might end up going to jail if I do see him." She turns away and stares at the wall again. I say, "I have no idea who the guy really is, but…"

"Jack," she cuts me off, "it's really him. It's really dad."

I can't believe she says that, and it pisses me off so much that she calls him dad. "What are you talking about, Sara? The guy is clearly nuts."

She looks away, then back at me. "Mom must have lied to us. It makes sense—all of the letters—they were from him." She stares at my face for a moment, studying my features. "He even looks like you."

I go home that night and start drinking.

I also made Sara tell me where the letters were in her room, so I got them out of her drawer and read every one of them.

62

I took some pills that night, and you already know I had too much to drink. So it shouldn't be surprising that I had the most vivid, extended dream that night that felt so real I wondered if it was more a drug-mixing hallucination.

If you were wondering, this is where you enter the story.

That's right.

You. Never would've guessed it, huh?

I just didn't know that it was *you*.

I wake up from numbness in the dream, then crawl out of some trench and onto burning hot sand. My mouth is cotton, my throat scratchy wool. Water the only thing on my mind.

I look to the right and you are with me, though I still can't make out your blurry face. You wipe the sleep from your eyes. "I wish we would have slept longer," you say. "Unconsciousness is the most appealing thing I've found here."

"We're up now, so we might as well try," I answer. "Maybe today will be a different story?" You look at me like you expect another long, despairing day in the desert and no more. So I look away from you and your unflagging realism.

We jog across burning sand to get to the marketplace. People are already mulling around, going from vendor to vendor, lines filling up. Some are already lying on the sand, writhing about and moaning from delusion. I know a few of them and feel very sorry, but what am I to do?

"What do you want to try first?" I ask.

"I don't know," you say. "How much money do you have?" We both pull out everything we had in our pockets and joined efforts. A few dozen coins.

The first merchant we walk by yells at the height of his ability: "Over here, over here! Sure-fire water is found over here! Look at the long line and see for yourself, we do not disappoint! Only one coin per cup!" I look at him and the taste in my mouth goes from dry to sour. The people in that line—I pity them. It stays packed every day, because part of what he says is right. Each cup does have a small drop of liquid in it—enough for you to forget about your misery for just a minute. But it is a quick, fleeting moment, and your mouth smacks horribly after tasting it, more dry and thirsty than before. So most people set their cup down and go right back to the back of the line, hour after hour, day after day.

"He is a liar—" I say. "Don't listen to him. I know this line well."

You look at me with sad eyes. "Jack, I've got to try something. I can't take this much longer." I frown and sit down to wait while you stand in line. When you get to the front I watch you put the cup to your mouth. One deep breath, then your head shakes violently and your teeth chatter. You walk to the back of the line, lips still smacking, but I get up and push you out of line and pull you along. You fight me for a second but soon give in and mope along behind me.

The next table we see is a man in a gloriously decorated booth with the latest gadgets and a $100 haircut. "Here, here!" he yells. "New product today—shiny, guaranteed to be effective!" His line is shorter because he was expensive. We stand in line and get to the front.

"Hey—hey you." I try to get his attention. "You say this is guaranteed?"

"Yes, guaranteed!" he yells, still talking to the crowd and not me.

"Look me in the eyes and tell me that..." I say. He flinches and repeats his line like a parrot—"New product, guaranteed to quench your thirst!"

"Hey!" I yell. "Look me in the damn eyes and tell me that!" I stare him down.

"Guaranteed!" he says again, to no one in particular.

"How much?" you ask. He tells us how much, and we cringe. Counting our coins, we decide to share one and handed him the money. You grab the cup and turn it up, then hand it to me. Not water—but a powdery white substance fills my quivering mouth. In an instant we are both lying on the ground, eyes rolled to the backs of our heads, numb to our very existence. Oblivious to the raging thirst, we sink into an artificial delight. After a few minutes of solace, I wake from my stupor and stand up, bent over my knees and huffing. You get up, sand still stuck to your face. "That didn't last as long as I had hoped," you say. A tear forms on the corner of your eyelid.

"I told you—" the vendor yells in our general direction, "I do not disappoint!"

There are some people yelling and making a fuss right ahead, so I stop the ringleader and ask, "What's all the fuss about?"

"I'm trying to convince these people to stop wasting their money on these liars!" He speaks passionately, red-faced.

"None of these people have any water to sell—they are cheats and frauds."

"Well—" you perk up, looking at him. "Do you have any water?"

He swallows and grinds his bottom lip with his teeth. "No," he finally says. We both look at him, confused. He is antsy, shuffling his feet about in the sand. Mouth dry and sticky.

"Well, I hate to be forward, sir," I said, "but at least those people have something for sale. Even if it isn't water." He huffs at me and kicks the sand around, staring at his feet. Then he wanders away, ranting and screaming at other unfortunate people.

We walk on, past more who are passed out on the ground, wriggling about, dying of thirst.

You look at me, wrinkling your forehead, and say, "I really don't want to end up like them…"

"Me either," I say, stepping over one of their legs.

We come to the next vendor. You wanted to lie down and take a rest, so I scope the place out. The vendor looks to have many clients of differing interests, so I hop in line and wait. In front of me stands a young girl who evidently doesn't think she is pretty, because she keeps watching men to study their reactions to her. She has darting eyes, and I feel sorry for her and want her to find some sort of relief. Behind me stands a desperate guy who keeps muttering, "I don't measure up, I don't measure up…" over and over, under his breath. We don't speak—you rarely do in those lines. Just keep moving forward with every customer who makes their transaction. I finally got to the front of the line.

"How much?" I ask.

"Seven coins," the merchant replies, smiling and looking past me.

I look down to my hand, sadly. "I only have four…" You have the bulk of the money with you and I have forgotten. I close my hand and start to walk away, until he grabs me by the shoulder. "Son…son—for you only I will make a special deal today. Four coins and that cup is yours!" I see a glimmer of hope and slide my coins into his hand. He gives me a cup and I turn it up as quickly as you'd expect. Sand fills my mouth and I fall to all fours, choking and spitting up the grit, trying to find saliva in my mouth to rid me of the feeling. Tears come to my eyes and I look at the merchant in disgust, while he grins back.

After a moment, I work up my strength, get up, and walk over to sit down where you are.

"Are you okay?" you ask.

"Yeah, I think so," I say, still spitting sand from my mouth. "I'm starting to get dizzy, though."

"Hey—do you know anything about that man over there, yelling in the distance?" I look up to where your gaze is pointing.

"No, I don't," I answer. We ask around and get some answers from different people:

"It's a mirage. He's not real."

"Only there to make fun of our misery. To give us false hope, then crush it."

"Someone I know tried it, and came back attesting that it wasn't a mirage. They were still disappointed, though. Said it's a lie. That there's a catch."

"The merchants discourage us from trying to go. They say the sand is too hot between here and there."

We get up and start walking again, past another tent. The vendor there screams loudly, and his line is long. But we see the result of his product, as customers touch the cup to their lips and drop motionless to the sand.

You stop cold and look away. "Do you want to at least walk out there? To see for ourselves if it's real?" You look out toward the screaming man. I can barely see him. "After all, what's one more mirage?"

"I don't think I can make it," I say, trying to steady myself. "I'm getting worse by the minute."

"I'll carry you if you don't make it," you say. You have such kind eyes. "Let's at least try."

We start half-running, stumbling across the fiery ground beneath us that burns hotter than summer pavement. I can finally hear the man yelling.

"Come, everyone who thirsts, come to the waters; and he who has no money, come, buy and eat! Come, buy wine and milk without money and without price. Why do you spend your money for that which is not bread, and your labor for that which does not satisfy? Listen diligently to me, and eat what is good, and delight yourselves in rich food. Incline your ear, and come to me; hear, that your soul may live!"

His voice is piercing—loud and confident.

"Let the one who is thirsty come! Let the one who desires take the water of life without price! Taste and see that the Lord is good! To the hungry, even the bitter tastes sweet."

A little less than halfway there I faint and collapse on the ground.

Sand fills my mouth and I am sure I am going to pass out. Next thing I know I am being carried along, hunched over your back, watching your legs slowly plow on, fading in and out.

The man still screams: "As when a hungry man dreams he is eating and awakes with his hunger not satisfied, or as when a thirsty man dreams he is drinking and awakes faint, with his thirst not quenched, so shall the multitude of all the nations be that fight against Mount Zion! Drink your fill from this fountain and you'll need no other!"

We get there soon enough, but there is a customer in front of us. I catch most of his speech.

"Listen," the man says. "I have heard that you really do have water. And I am here, once again, to buy some from you." He set down a large bag of coins on the table. "I will excuse your rudeness from the past, and I assure you that what I have brought today is more than ever—that there is more money in this bag than you have ever seen in your life. Surely this will meet your price."

He is the man from earlier who was shouting in the streets about liars and frauds.

I can't see him, but I hear the merchant vaguely. "Friend, just like I told you yesterday and the day before and the day before. My water is not for sale. You will not acquire it by bargaining. If you want it, all you need is need. All you need is nothing."

"How dare you insult me once again," the man responds, indignant. "Everything has a price, and I am a man of means. Who are you to tell me what I can and cannot buy?"

"Just like you've heard over and over," the merchant says calmly. "This water is only for the despairing beggar. It cannot be bought by any price. He who has ears, let him hear."

"Nonsense!" the man yells. "My ears work fine, I assure you. They just know nonsense when they hear it. I guess your water is not fit for me anyway, for I am neither despairing nor a beggar. I am a man of dignity and self-respect. Nevertheless, I will gather more money, and I will be back later with an offer you cannot refuse."

With that, he grabs his sack of coins in haste and stomps off, smacking his mouth in a thirsty disgust.

The merchant then turns to you.

"Hello there, friend. Have you come for water?"

"Yes—I guess I have," you stammer, laying me down on the ground. You continue, "In all my life I've never seen anything be free. People always, always want something for what they have to offer. So I have heard that there is a catch to this water that makes people turn around without drinking, and I can't imagine that there isn't. But sir, I'm afraid I am at the end of my rope and you are my only hope. And even worse, I have no money—what little I had left fell out of my pocket on the way here, when I bent down to pick him up—" I try to look up and get a better gauge on what is happening. "So I ask sir, if there is any way I can meet the require- ments or get around the catch and get some of your water?" I try to turn my head to look, but am not strong enough.

"Please," you continue. "What is the catch?"

"You people have been burned so much," the man says. "You call it a catch—I call it grace. Do you want to know what you have to do to get my water?"

"Yes, I do. I really do," you say. My throat aches.

"Nothing. Absolutely nothing!" he says. "This living water is offered to you freely, and you will never thirst again. You have come here, knowing that you can't pay for this water or earn it on your own, which is true. But I have paid for it and I offer it to you without price. There is no amount I would accept for it other than nothing, and you have come to me with gloriously empty hands. Look at them!" he says, looking at your outstretched hands. "Now pick up that jug and drink your fill."

Something hits me inside, and I awake enough to look up and gain a bit of clarity. You look at me, I look at the merchant, and a chill sputters up my stomach and into my throat.

"No—don't!" I yell to you. "Don't listen to him!" I start to cry from despair. "I know him and he is as fake as it gets—a bigger liar than all of the merchants combined. Don't even waste your en- ergy reaching out—it's just going to crumble to dust in your hands."

Yeshua stands there, bearded and dressed in his homeless clothes. His eyes are wet, a quivering smile on his face. He holds out a tall glass pitcher, clear water gushing over the sides.

I bury my head in my hands. "They were right—"

"Jack," you interrupt. "He is looking me in the eyes. No one has done that yet. They are as still as stones."

"He's a good liar," I say. "And besides, even if he wasn't fake —I would rather die than drink water from him."

He steps toward me, a tear trailing down his cheek, jug of water still in hand. I am on my knees.

"Jack," he says. "I am so very sorry for the innumerable ways that I have hurt you. I am a broken man and I will let you down—but I promise you this water is real—as real as the raging thirst in your throat. I wish someone else could offer it to you so it would be easier to take, but it is a task I have been given. So I beg you, son, drink. Drink freely." He holds the jug out in my direction.

I recoil, though enticed by the coldness of the water. "No. I can't trust you," I say, turning away. "Some burning bush you turned out to be." I try to spit on him, but I have no saliva in my mouth to expel.

"Jack, please, drink the water. You're going to die if you don't." His face pleads with me.

"Why don't you just pour it out on the ground and laugh at me?" I ask. He says nothing in response, just moves an inch closer to me, still holding it out. It sloshes around and a few drops spill onto the sand, instantly soaked up. I want it so badly.

"At least let me pay for it so I won't have to take it from you."

He cocks his head to the side. "Jack, you know it doesn't work that way. Please. Drink."

He stops and pours a little water out on his left palm, letting it run through his fingers. "He satisfies the longing soul, and the hungry soul he fills with good things." He pauses and I watch the water drip from his hand to the sand below. "Taste and see, Jack. Taste and see."

I look at you, and you are crying too. I sit back, waiting on the cruel reveal to the joke.

He continues, "Jack, I may be a fraud, and I'm sorry for that. But this water isn't. Please, son. Take it."

I wince and bend down, unable to produce tears from de-hydration. Something snaps in me and I reach up quickly and put my hands around the cold glass. The cold sides do not turn to dust, and my fingers jolt at the relief that comes from just holding it. I quickly turn the jug up all the way to my mouth.

"Yes, drink! Drink freely!" He yells, grinning and bursting into a full, raucous laugh.

Cold, clear water rushes into my mouth and down my throat, gulp after gulp. The most infinite, penetrating relief reaches down to my bones, and I manage a smile as I drink the last drop in the jug.

63

I woke up Friday morning and called in sick to work. And I was—I was sick to my stomach. So I had a few beers for breakfast. Then a few more for a mid-morning snack.

There are mean drunks, and nice drunks, and funny drunks. I've already told you I can be a silly drunk or an emotional drunk. I'll let you guess what I was that day. I pretty much just drank and napped all day in the dark apartment, watching awful cable TV shows whenever I would wake up. I woke up that night around eight and realized that I had slept through Sara's visitation hours. I could have punched myself, but instead I just drank some more and went to sleep.

Sara called me on Saturday morning and left me a voicemail while I was in the shower:

"Jack. I missed you last night. I hope everything is okay. Hey, I hate to ask you this, and I know are not going to want to. If you don't, that's okay. But...will you please bring him to visit tomorrow? I just have something I need to tell him, and I really want to do it in person. My counselor said I need to get everything inside of me out." I cursed under my breath.

"Okay, I'll see you tomorrow regardless. Bye."

I slammed the phone down on the table. After I dressed I went to the refrigerator and opened a beer and almost chugged it. I sat down on the couch for a while, staring into space. Fortunately, I couldn't honor Sara's request.

I had no idea where the man lived.

64

Sunday morning I woke up and found myself driving to the coffee shop without even realizing it.

Man, was I out of it.

I realized it on the way there, but decided to just go along with it, grab myself a bagel and take the morning to get out of the apartment and just think. Maybe outline a plan for finding a place where I can keep the boys on the weekends. Maybe figure out how I'm going to survive in a post-Chloe universe. Maybe just plan the next few columns.

I got there, stood in line, ordered my bagel, and turned to sit.

And froze.

There he was, in our usual spot, a Bible open in front of him, reading away.

My head swam and my stomach dropped to the floor. He was clean-shaven, out of his homeless attire and in everyday clothes. And then he looked up and saw me.

Then I stood there, silent, rocking back and forth, just a couple steps away from where we had spent so many Sunday mornings.

There we were, for who knows how long, just looking at each other.

And for some reason, I sat down.

"How is Sara doing?" he asked.

I closed my eyes.

"Who the hell do you think you are?" I said. "You think you just get to show up and suddenly care about Sara and me again?"

"Jack...it's not—" he stopped himself, breathing deeply. "I'm sorry."

"I wish you knew how pitiful those words sound," I whispered through my teeth, trying to keep my composure in the coffee shop. "How hollow and weak and asinine—"

"I know," he said, furrowing his brow and looking down at his Bible. "I know. There is nothing I can say."

"Actually, there is. Tell me everything," I said, folding my arms. I didn't know what else to say.

"When I left that night," he said, and perhaps the weight of what he was about to do caught up to him, because he sat there for a moment, staring at me. "When I walked out on your mother, you, and Sara, I was the most pitiful, selfish, miserable son of a bitch you could ever imagine. I screwed around for a couple of years and did a lot of stupid, stupid things. I know you thought I had vanished, but I was around. I went to baseball games and watched you run around. I rode by the playground and watched you chase Sara and laugh. I sat in the back at school plays. I was an invisibly proud father.

"I talked to Mom on and off, though she obviously hid that from you. You might not believe this, but there was a time when I started to come to my senses, and I talked to her a lot. She was seriously thinking about taking me back and trying to work things out. I don't know why, but she was.

"That was right around the time she found out about Uncle Richard. She blamed me for it. If I would have stuck around, there would have been no need for a babysitter. She was right. And I'll never, ever forgive myself for that.

"I had already messed up so much, and I knew I couldn't fix what had already happened to you. And faced with a future without you, without Sara, without your mom—I killed him, Jack. I put my gun right between his eyes as he pleaded for his life, and his brains splattered on the wall. I ransacked the house to make it look like a burglary gone wrong, then left. But I couldn't run forever.

"I confessed to the judge and cried like a baby telling him the story. He found some legal loophole and reduced my charge to second degree. I served sixteen years. I know your mom told you that I was dead, and she wrote me in jail asking me to promise to never let you know any different. Said you didn't deserve to be hurt anymore. But she sent me letters and pictures of you two occasionally while I was in prison. I hung them up all over my cell and told anyone who would listen about you two.

"About eight years in I was really depressed, and even tried to commit suicide a few times. Being in jail makes that somewhat hard to accomplish. That's when I started reading the Bible and somehow, though I'm still not sure when or how it happened, I met Jesus. Not, you know, in person, like I wanted you to believe. But I met him nonetheless.

"I got out around three years ago, just a few weeks before your mother died in that accident. I was at the funeral, standing in the back. Knowing that all of this mess was my fault."

I stared at my unappetizing food, fighting back tears and trying not to look at him. He paused for a minute and then went on.

"I've followed you and Sara since, Jack. That's how I knew about the affair. I was the guy on the other aisle in the grocery store. The guy sitting four rows behind you at the movies. The man walking around in the park during your picnic. I've watched Isaac and Liam grow taller, wilder, and cuter, if that's even possible."

My head was swirling with questions and thoughts and emotions—I couldn't possibly keep them all straight.

"There have been a million ways I've thought up to come clean with you," he said. "I almost went through with it a couple of times. I threw away a lot of letters. In the end I always decided that you two were better off not knowing—that I had inflicted enough pain on your lives, that you each had gotten over it and that reconnecting would only make things worse. That I didn't even deserve the opportunity for you to spit in my face and tell me to go to hell.

"I've always been worried about Sara. The letter you saw—I wrote that. I wrote all of them. It was the only way I could come up with to try to help her. When I found out about Jordan I started to worry more about you. And then I read your article, and I decided I had to do something. I devoted my life that week to concocting the most insanely ridiculous idea I've ever heard. I didn't even sleep. I wanted to help you see the truth and I didn't know how else to do it, so I was willing to risk everything. If I could pull it off, then I could vanish without a trace, hopefully after helping you get your family back. It was the most fun and significant thing I have ever done in my life, and potentially one of the most irresponsible and stupid. But I have to be honest—I would be lying if I said that part of the motivation wasn't getting to spend this precious time with you. My son that I don't deserve."

I raised my head and glared at him. "Don't you dare," I said. "Don't you dare call me your *son*." The words cut him, and I was glad.

He didn't budge. "I am so sorry, Jack. Everything I have ever done has hurt you."

I stood up. "I don't care." I went and tossed my uneaten breakfast in the trash. And against my better judgment, I turned back to him and told him to meet me at Three Rivers for visiting hours that night. I did it for Sara. But I hoped against hope that he wouldn't show.

65

He was waiting outside Three Rivers when I pulled up.

"Hey Jack," he said as I approached. He was very clammy and sweaty.

We went inside and signed in. While putting on our name tags, he coughed and looked up at me, red-faced. "Any idea what to expect here? I'm a little nervous."

I considered not answering, but then I had a better idea. "If I know Sara, I would be prepared for the worst."

It's not like he didn't deserve the worst.

We were escorted back to the same room I'd been in a few nights before, and so we sat down and waited. He kept wiping his hands on his pants and tapping his foot on the floor.

A few long minutes went by, and then the door opened and in walked Sara in her blue hoodie, followed by a few employees in scrubs and her counselor. Sara's eyes went straight for him and we stood up, but then she stopped in the middle of the room and just stood there. Someone closed the door. The man who called himself our father caught his breath, and we endured an excruciating silence, standing there like zombies. Her eyes hadn't left his, and he was starting to tear up.

"Sara—" he said, then heaved a deep sigh.

"Hey, sweetheart." She stood still and silent, her eyes burning into him.

"Whatever it is you're feeling—" he went on, sniffling and wiping his pants again. "You can let it all out honey. I promise—I know I deserve it. I don't even deserve the chance to stand here and be yelled at by you, so whatever you need to say is—"

She stepped forward, stopping him mid-sentence. About a foot or so in front of him, she hesitated and her eyes watered up. Then she reached up with both arms and put them around his neck and laid her head on his shoulder.

"Thank you," she said. "Thank you." She stepped back for a minute and looked at him. "For all of the letters. You saved my life more than once—"

She hugged him again and I thought he was going to fall down in the floor he wept so hard, his arms pressing into the back of her sweatshirt. His hands almost turned white, he squeezed her so hard.

"Sara, I am so, so sorry..." he said, over and over as he sobbed.

66

When we were leaving that night, I stopped him right before he was about to get in his truck.

"Hey—" I said, "Just because she hugged you, that doesn't mean we can just be a happy little family again."

He looked at me and pain crept through the joy in his eyes. "I know, Jack. I know that. I will count any interaction I get with you two as a blessing and not a right. I promise you that." He paused and looked at his feet, then back at me. "But I love you. And I will not stop loving you. I believe you might say it like this: *rivers and roads*." Another moment passed, then he started to walk away. "Bye, Jack," he said, waving.

"Hey—" I said, stopping him. I swallowed the hardness in my throat. "Thank you. For writing her those letters."

"I guess we share the joy of writing," he said with a sad smile. "But if I would have done my job as a father, there would have never been a need for those letters. So there's no need for thanks." He waved and walked away, jingling his keys.

67

I'm not really sure what to leave you with. My story is quite unfinished.

It's been almost a month since we went to visit Sara that night. I haven't spoken to him again since then. But thankfully, Sara is doing very well. I hope she will get to come home next week.

I'm still at the apartment, but I'm not too lonely anymore. I'm back at Recovery, trying to actually deal with my own issues this time. I have a lot. As if you didn't know that already. Sometime in the near future I hope to write a column about Ron, Luis, Frank and the others. If they let me, of course.

Maybe you want to hear about this:

Last Sunday night I was sitting on the couch watching a movie. It was raining hard outside, and I heard a loud rap on the door. I got up to see who it was, and lost my breath when I looked through the peephole.

"Chloe?"

"Hey, Jack," she said. Her hair was wet and she held some kind of paper in her hand.

"Come on in—"

"No, I'm fine right here."

She looked around and then back at me, taking a small step backwards.

"What's going on?" I asked, stepping out onto the porch with her. She paused for a moment, then held up the piece of paper.

"He wrote me and told me the whole story, Jack—your dad." She swallowed and looked down at the boards beneath us, then up at me. "That is insane."

"I know," I said. "Ridiculous."

"Have you seen him since then?" she asked.

I told her about breakfast that Sunday, and visiting Sara. We talked a bit more about the whole story, filling in the gaps that he hadn't told her.

"Well, I just wanted to stop by and tell you that I knew, and say, well—I don't really know what to say," she said. "Wow."

"Thanks, Chloe. Thanks for coming by."

"Yeah," she said. "Well...bye, Jack." She started to walk away.

"Chloe—" I said, and she stopped to look back my way. "I'm not really sure how else I can put myself out there and beg for a second chance, without just embarrassing you more—but I was just wondering...have you considered it lately?"

She bit her lip, then answered quickly.

"No."

I stepped back with my right foot and felt her sharpness stab me. "So if I got down on one knee and proposed to you right here...?" I joked.

"Not a chance," she said, without looking at me. She stood there and I didn't know quite what to do. I expected her to just walk off any second. I just wanted to lie down on the floor and cry.

It was really awkward, so I continued the helpless and pitiful joke. "So if I asked you out on a date...?"

She paused, eyes still not meeting mine:

"I think I'm free Saturday night."

It took a minute to sink in. "Yeah?"

She turned her back and spoke as she walked away. "I'm free Saturday night at seven. Don't be late to pick me up."

She's going on a date with me!

She's going on a date with me!

68

Today is Saturday, if you were wondering. In just a few hours I'm gonna go get ready and pick up my bride. I'm gonna take her to the restaurant we had our first married date at, then to dessert at Nonnah's, and if she's up for it, I want to drive out to the field in Lexington where we always used to go lay and look at the stars.

I love that woman so much more than I could ever write or say. Words just feel silly. I hope so badly that I get the chance to pursue her for the rest of my life, even though I don't deserve her.

Rivers and roads, Chloe. Rivers and roads.

I'm sitting here thinking, and part of me feels the urge to find him and thank him. I don't want to acknowledge it, but he got me a date with my wife. I'm scared to do that, however, because part of me wants to beat him senseless, and another big part of me wants to forget that he even exists and banish his very name from my memory.

But there is this nagging thought that he said he would help me however he could to have another chance with Chloe, and he somehow accomplished that with the letter he sent her—so I should at least thank him for that.

Even if I never see him again afterward.

What do you think?

I'm thinking not today. Maybe some other time.

You know that I'm different now, one way or another. You may be wondering whether I've just gotten my head on straight, or if I've bought into the whole Jesus and gospel deal, fed to me by a fake Jesus and his cast of characters. The truth is, hell if I know. I'm still figuring that out myself.

But…you want to know something interesting?

I can sit still now. I'm not sure what that means, but I have never been able to sit still. Never. I have never really felt at home in my own skin.

Have you ever felt like that? Like a prisoner in your own restless body that tells you to get up, get a beer, turn on the TV, check Facebook, etc.?

I'm sure you have no idea what I'm talking about.

Unless you're human.

But now I can sit still, and it's the most remarkable thing. I just sit there and breathe, in and out, in and out. Quiet. I don't even mind the quiet now. The frantic searching to entertain or occupy or distract myself is gone. I don't necessarily even need coffee or a beer, although sometimes they can add to the experience. It really is incredible, though I'm afraid it falls into that category where words just fail to describe it. You'd have to feel it to know it.

I didn't tell you the end of my dream.

After turning the jug up, I crawl on my knees for a few feet in the sand, then manage to stand up, still wiping the water from my face. I feel clearer and stronger already, the dehydration quickly fading away. Something pokes my toes, and I look down to see grass sprouting through the sand, sucking it away and raising my feet under a smooth green carpet. I look to my right and see the most beautiful river rush into existence, waves and ripples crawling on each other downstream. Trees and bushes and flowers sprout and I have to brace myself to keep from falling down. A large oak picnic table comes to life.

Somehow I realize that this place wasn't changing—I was the one who was changing. Beholding things that were always there and I could never see.

Seated at the picnic table are Luis, Frank, Allen, Ron, Willie, and others. And, you are not going to believe this—my mom is there. Her hair radiates brightness as she laughs, cocking her head back in some grand joy. They are eating this massive spread of food, drinking glasses of wine and laughing at Luis, who is very expressively telling some story. It's clear that they love each other in the deepest kind of way, and it is so attractive. I exhale and laugh and turn to run to them, but stop before I take a step.

Because there you are, still standing there in the hot sand, the line of grass halfway between us.

"Are you coming?" I ask.

You look at me with a tangible despair in your eyes, then back at the person standing in front of you. But instead of Yeshua, my father, it is someone else standing there, holding out the jug of water to you, begging you to take it.

I don't know who it is—their features are fuzzy and indistinct—but judging from your tears, you do.

Is it your mother? Your sister? Your father? Someone who hurt you in the past—a colleague or pastor or best friend? I don't know. I can't know. But I know that you are shaken to the core by what you see.

"Hey—it's okay," I say, stepping toward you. "I understand. It's not easy to forgive. But it's worth it. It's worth it to try. It's not a mirage. It's real."

You look at me again and more tears drip off of your face and fall to the sand below. You stand there, trying to decide if you can trust, if you can accept this offer from this person from your past standing there, holding out the water to you.

It breaks my heart.

"Come on," I say, reaching out to you with my hand. "I'll help you."

I don't know why you are in my dream.

But I know there is a reason. And I kind of get this weird feeling that maybe my story is more for you than it is for me. That it is something I am supposed to share with you, and that it is really important that I do so. I don't know how much I can help, but I would love to try if you want. I would love to work through this together somehow and figure out things as we go. I hope that when I give this story to you it won't be the last time I hear from you. I really do.

If you think I'm crazy, that's okay. That doesn't worry me as much as it used to. And if you aren't buying all this, I understand. I'd just hate so badly for you to finally find the source of joy we are all looking for, and it turn out to be the one place you refuse to take it from. Flawed souls can still speak truth, I've learned.

I'm going to save this on my USB drive, get up, introduce myself, and give it to you on the way out. I hope you don't throw it away.

I'll be here next week at the exact same time if you want to talk about your ending to the story. And if you want, I can give you an update on Sara and Chloe.

I hope your tired eyes find the peace they are looking for.

For your sake, I hope you drink the water.

The End

Note From the Author

I'm not sure how you stumbled upon this book, but I'm glad you did. I know there will be a myriad of "you's" that find themselves as the recipients of this story, and just as many responses to it. And that's okay, because I wrote it for every single one of you. And I hope that it at least, in some small way poked you in the eye, where you will at least have to walk away and think or struggle with something. Because that's what stories are for.

First of all, I know this was a story, but I meant what I said. I intended to write it, not for a vacuum, but to start genuine conversations with real people…real "you's". I hope to receive emails from some of you, meet some of you, get coffee with some of you, etc. If you'd like to share your thoughts or response with me, feel free to email me at: brandon@everybushisburning.com.

You can also connect with me at the website, and there is even a place for you to respond by writing your own ending to the story, whether figuratively in the dream scene or just a general response to the story…maybe what you would say if you could have coffee with Jack. You can also listen to some of the music mentioned in the story on the website. So enjoy that if you want. Jack likes some pretty good music after all…

Secondly, I want to say that although this is, of course, a made up story—there are also real people present within these pages. Most of the characters from Midtown are real people, and their stories are true. Ron, Luis, Frank, Willie, Edmond—they are all very real. I know this because I have the privilege of sharing life with them and leading the Recovery ministry that was a part of the story. I put them and their real stories and names in the story for three reasons. First, because they allowed me to. Secondly, because they are better than anything I could make up. And lastly, because most every time I get to the end of a novel I wish that at least some of the characters were actually real, because I want to meet them. So, in light of that, I am privileged to introduce you to some of my friends. I hope to get to write more about their stories soon.

The pastors that played a role in the story are all real. They helped start the church family that I call home, which also happens to be the environment in which God has restored my hope for the American church. I've been blessed to be part of good churches before, but seeing the picture of gospel-centered family that God has graciously grown in us has wrecked me in the best way.

As you probably have guessed, Jack's character is a reflection of myself in many ways. Especially in the sense that, despite an unwavering commitment to Jesus, I have gone through periods of severe disenchantment with the way Jesus is often represented by American Christianity. This book was birthed out of that disenchantment, along with a desire to apologize for the things with the Christian label that have muddied Jesus' name, including, of course, the innumerable failures and shortcomings of myself and other imperfect followers of Jesus. I can only hope that this book has helped to clear a little of the mud—for one person or hopefully a bunch of people.

Thanks again for sharing this story with me. And I really mean what I said—I'd love to hear from you.

www.EveryBushIsBurning.com

P.S. During the last months of writing this story, Willie Smith, Jr. passed away. He was tragically killed on February 26th, 2011. Willie was a dear part of our church family and he is sorely missed.

Acknowledgements

I am incredibly blessed with family, friends, and support...so this is going to take a while.

First, to my wife Kristi. For more conversations and ideas than I could ever count. For your unending encouragement and support, and for your honesty. Couldn't have done this without you. I love living life with you, babe.

Next, to Andy Meisenheimer, my editor. I am truly embarrassed to think about what this book would be like without your involvement. Thanks for believing in this story and pushing me, for your really long emails back in the day, and for making me a better writer. You are very good at what you do.

I have some extremely talented friends who put in a ton of work to help make this project a reality, and I am incredibly indebted to them. To Jeremy Lethco and Austin Grebenc from Dust of the Ground Media—thanks for the incredible trailer. Your creativity and talent amaze me, and I am so thankful for the amazingly cool video that I hope will help this story catch fire. Thanks for going above and beyond, and Jeremy—I am ever appreciative of your friendship, as well as your insight and encouragement in this.

To Kent Bateman, for all the time and sweat you put into making a really cool cover and website design, and for your feedback and ideas for the book. You are a talented dude and I am so grateful to call you a friend. To Stephen Bateman, thanks for building us an awesome website and for all of your advice. You have a very bright future ahead of you and I'm excited to see what the Lord does through you.

Matt Crawford—thanks for your interest, encouragement, and ideas, as well as your help with proofreading. I've been incredibly thankful for you throughout this entire process. Speaking of proofreading, thanks for your help Sean Brereton. It's good to have you back from Seattle.

Greg Darley—thanks for shepherding me through this process and for your passion and inspiration. Thanks for spurring me on to get through the difficult parts. Your ambition and drive have been an inspiration to me.

Travis Wright and Matt Shearer—thanks for your early encouragement, honesty and feedback. You guys really helped me push through and I am so grateful for your support. Matt, thanks for that day in Cool Beans when you read the ending and for your help with proofreading.

Lee Cunningham, thanks for your all the front porch talks, and for your wisdom and encouragement. You are a dear friend and I am so thankful for your support through this project. Jon Ludovina, thanks for unmerited encouragement on a pretty terrible early draft that I needed to keep going. Thanks for what you told me in Immac that day—it was enough encouragement to get through a major revision.

Adam and Courtney Gibson, thanks for cooking us dinner that night and giving me your very helpful and specific feedback. You guys caught several things that I am so thankful for.

Michael Bailey and Jay Hendricks—thanks for all the conversations through the years, and for your feedback on the story. Bailey, thanks for Monterrey's that night, and Jay, thanks for following me home and celebrating on the front porch that day the first copies came in. Dustin Willis, thanks for your support and advice through this project—for being on my team as you said. That means a lot. Thanks for telling me I could come intern at Midtown when I was a dumb college student that you didn't even know.

Mom, thanks for reading and giving honest feedback—your perspective helped a lot. And of course, thanks for being the best mom in the world. But that goes without saying. And Dad, Hannah & Mema, thanks for being the best. Love you so much.

To all my friends who I gave *Bathing Jesus* to years ago (in the black binders)—thanks and I'm sorry. I know it was terrible. To Chris Brown, thanks for actually reading the entire thing, making meticulous notes and taking me to Village Idiot to give me feedback. I cannot tell you how encouraging that was, and I will never forget it.

To Ron, Luis, Frank, Edmond, and Willie—thanks for letting me share you with the world. I love all of you guys dearly and I'm thankful for your friendship. And Willie—we all miss you. Terribly. Columbia is truly not the same without you.

To early beta readers, thank you so much. Courtney Tipping. Renie Willis. Beth Kay. Josh & Alice Garrett. Ashley Wright. Melissa Fennel. Ann Marie Amick. Joe Hanaan. Alex and Andrew Gilstrap. Katie Brewer. Galen and Michael McAneney. Frank Dempsey. Tyler Macchio. Josh Cox. Jeff Jacobs. Toni Lawrimore.

Sarah Cunningham and Stephen Brewster—thanks for your advice and encouragement when you had just met me at the STORY lunch in Charlotte. That meant a lot to me. Chad Gibbs—thanks for lunch at Hunter Gatherer and for giving your time to a young, wannabe writer. Anne Jackson—thanks for your advice and encouragement when I talked to you at Catalyst. You gave me a lot of courage to do this thing on my own.

Last but certainly not least—thanks to my Midtown family. Thanks for striving to be a Jesus-centered family on mission. We all know we are far from perfect, but Jesus is working here in our family to make the gospel more prevalent and foundational to everything. I hope this story gives people at least a small picture of how good and beautiful biblical community can be. What we have has been described as special, but let's hope and pray that what we have spreads so much that it won't be special anymore.

Kickstarter Supporters

To all of my Kickstarter backers…we did it! Thanks so much for pitching in to make this project a reality, and I can't say how much I appreciate each and every one of you. It's been so incredible to accomplish this with your help.

Eric & Ginny Moulton
Bobby & Amber Moore
Landon & Jordan Thompson
Michael Bailey
Jon & Erica Ludovina
Joshua Story
Matt & Sara Crawford
Kent Bateman
Jay & Liza Hendricks
Dean & Meagan Chanter
Josh & Alice Garrett
Lucy Bascom
Ann Melton
Lee & Pam Clements
Hannah Clements
Mark & Dephanie Caldwell
Ron & Judy Gilstrap
Courtney & Adam Gibson

Matt & Jennifer Davis
Meghan Wohleber
Billy & Elizabeth Tipping
Allen & Courtney Tipping
Georgina Wilson
Stephen Bateman
Kevin & Kim Gilstrap
Ginger Holland
Jonathan & Carmen Stone
Traylor & Hannah Disbrow
Lois Melton
Greg & Crystal Hair
Jeff Hsiang
Galen McAneney
Jen Beres
Kenny Dorian
Stephanie Bikcen
Thor Sawin
Heather Mossop
Anna Gray Macmurphy
April Gibson
Travis & Ashley Wright
Kristie Flynn
Matt Rollison
Drew Mendoza
Brittany Stevens
Stephanie Redmond
Michael McAneney
Ruth Resce Devroomen
Andrew Yuhas
Chris Molony
Tim Jones
Sara Prothro
Ryan Rike
LK Callicott
Lisa Bloomer

Bonnie Powell

Greg & Betsey Darley

Matt & Shannon Robertson

Anita Alverson

Charlie & Debbie Gibbs

Gary Price

Julie Orr

Ashley Bowman

Jill Webb

Tom Walsh

Sue Caldwell

Taylor Huettig

Jonathan Williams

Alex Gilstrap

Harriett Lappin

Caitlin Storck

Pate McKissack

Jim & Jane Hendricks

Benny Holland

Bill Holland

CPSIA information can be obtained at www.ICGtesting.com
Printed in the USA
BVOW032252201211

278872BV00002B/2/P